The
Jack Newton
Radio

Jon Lawrence

This book was first published in 2017 by Create Space
for Little Eden Books
First edition 2017.
© 2017 Jon Lawrence / Little Eden Books
Little Eden Books
Keepers Cottage
Low Road
Walpole Cross Keys
King's Lynn
Norfolk
PE34 4HA

ISBN:1533407355
ISBN-13:9781533407351

DEDICATION

This book is lovingly dedicated to my dear, late mother Margaret Karen Lawrence. Wherever you are I hope this book goes a little way to making up for my shortcomings.

Love you x

CONTENTS

ACKNOWLEDGMENTS

I would like to thank the following people for their help, kindness, support and inspiration throughout the writing of this novel:

Alexis Ffrench, Donna Reid, Annette De Vanche, Sarah Chalke, Sandy & Claire Mears, Nik Gamble, Stef Judd, Chris Skinner, Brian Eno, Gerald Finzi, Thomas Newman, Max Richter, Roger Eno, Alan Rickman, Bliss, Alan Silvestri, Barrington Pheloung, Arvo Part and, of course, my lovely family – Kerry-Ann, Hayden & Austin.

Love to all at *The Big C* Cancer Support Group.

Special thanks to all at Denver Primary.

1
Driving Home

Everything was moving faster than Anwyn Jones and Byron. Cars, trucks, motorbikes and coaches all sped past her as she ambled at forty-five miles-per-hour along the M4 motorway, in her 1966 Morris Minor Traveller. Byron, a wire-haired Jack Russell terrier, stood his front paws on the armrest and stared inquisitively at the world outside. The gulls gliding alongside the motorway seemed to leave Anwyn behind, and even the white clouds appeared to be abandoning her and racing off to meet the horizon as the sun fell into the west. Faster still, was life itself. It seemed to go at a steady speed forty years ago, when a year felt like a year. Yet, as she tootled cautiously along the inside lane, she felt the ticks and tocks of her life slipping away faster than the white dotted lines at the side of the road.

Her mother always told her that time was a great healer, but with each passing day she began to consider it more of a death sentence. Time was no friend to Anwyn. She hated it and resented it. The more she had appreciated life, with all of its love and nuanced beauty, the more time seemed to be taking it away. It took contemporaries, friends who had walked with her through the good and the bad, it took her abilities of concentration and memory, and physical faculties – fading eyesight, the aches and pains of Arthritis in her joints, as well as slight hearing loss.

Since the loss of Michael, her husband of over forty years, the world seemed to have lost all of its colour. She only seemed to notice the grey skies, while blue summer days went almost unnoticed. Sunrises and sunsets, which she loved to watch with Michael, seemed somehow less vibrant, the hues watered down and bland. Grief forced Anwyn to look at the world through different eyes. Her ears too, could no longer detect the sound of melodious music. The radio had not worked in the car for years. Long holiday drives with Michael had been filled with the soothing sound of familiar conversation. The sweet song of the blackbird in the garden, the tunes of sparrows, blue tits, wrens, goldfinches and robins around the birdfeeder and the midnight hoots of the tawny owl in the woods at the end of their garden had long since gone, only to be replaced by the raucous squawks of the carrion crows and jackdaws. Tastes had also been affected. Nobody on earth could make an earl grey tea like Michael – not even Anwyn herself. Sweet cakes and gentle spices, in all their culinary forms were replaced by an ever-present bitterness. The moon was never full and the sun always seemed to cast a shadow before her.

The road to St David's, the smallest city in the UK, and the most westerly city in Wales, never seemed to end. Around each bend there seemed to be little more than… another bend. After a while, the energetic Byron curled up his little white body in the foot-well and drifted off to sleep.

Once off the sterile motorway, A-roads led her through Carmarthen and Haverfordwest, until yet humbler roads guided her along the coast to her destination.

St David's had been her childhood home until the age of six, when her parents sent her off to a preparatory school in London. Her father, an austere general practitioner at the local health centre, had instilled a strong work ethic and a love of life rather than possessions. The house which they grew up in had remained in the family ever since. It had always been a simple existence, but a happy one, which Anwyn and Michael tried to continue into their own marriage. Possessions meant nothing, they were just *things*. The few material possessions which did hold any real value included the wedding rings, the books (of which there were hundreds) and the radio.

As Anwyn made her way along the last few miles of road which twisted toward St David's, the rain began to fall, softly at first and then with increasing force. The wipers struggled to clear the windscreen of the deluge, so she was forced to reduce her speed to a crawl. Anwyn gripped tightly on to the steering wheel, moved her face closer to the windscreen and squinted her eyes. As she made her final turning off the main road and on to a tiny dirt track, the moon played hide and seek behind the perpetual motion of storm clouds sweeping inland off the Irish and Celtic seas. The stony lane zigged and zagged down a cliff side and eventually led to a small white cottage. Nestled precariously into the cliff-side, the humble abode was open to the extreme elements. As her headlights illuminated the building, Anwyn saw that the faintly familiar cottage was in need of serious repair. The whiteness of the walls had been dulled by time and weather, while the paint on the window frames peeled and gnarled like the curved wooden shavings in a carpenter's workshop. The metal drainpipes had started to rust and black slate roof tiles had clearly loosened. It certainly didn't seem like the house that she had grown up in as a child, yet her initials, still carved into the gatepost, proved that it was so.

Anwyn rested her head on the steering wheel for a while as she waited for the rain to relent enough for her to unpack. Her long grey hair fell down softly as her eyes did their best to remain open. The headlights, still shining in the darkness, gently lit the raindrops outside. In her lassitude, she closed her eyes and heard the distant echo inside her head of her father's voice.

'Anwyn!' he called, 'You'll catch your death out there. Come in out of the rain and we'll do some reading.'

Anwyn opened her eyes as her father's echo diminuendoed back in her memory, and spoke softly.

'Okay, Daddy.'

After a little while the rain thinned out and Anwyn pulled herself out of the car, holding on to the frame of the door for support. Byron, his excitement renewed in these new surroundings, twisted and turned and jumped up at Anwyn, almost causing her to trip.

'Get down, you daft sod!' she hollered. 'You nearly made me fall flat on my arse!'

There were mercifully few belongings to bring in to the little house. A few bags, a couple of boxes and a collection of coats and blankets strewn over the back seat were all she had to unpack. Indeed, they were all she had – at all. The septuagenarian had these few possessions to show for her life as Michael's wife and personal secretary. Having moved from London in order to escape the noise, the violence and speed of the city, she whittled her belongings down to the bare essentials to begin her life again, this time without Michael. Michael had died a year ago following a massive stroke, which killed him almost instantly as he waited for a train at Euston Station. There had been no signs of illness prior to his passing and the shock and grief had, at times, proved too much for Anwyn. Tsunamis of sorrow would wash over her in a café, while waiting at a traffic light or while talking to somebody, leaving her unable to speak or move, paralysed by loneliness. These moments, although fleeting, were starting to become more and more common. She had no particular affiliation for London, or indeed anywhere. London (Islington, to be precise) was simply the place where she laid her head at the end of each day. Home was where Michael was.

Some weeks after Michael's passing, she felt the vastness of the city closing in on her, as it had never done before. The constant noises of the cars, music blaring out of shops and bars, the ever-shining neon lights and unnecessary streetlamps which polluted the natural night sky, and the smell of refuse piled high in back alleys had begun to assault her senses. She felt as though the concrete, asbestos, plastics and indeed all things unnatural were poisoning her – she couldn't breathe. She needed the open air. She yearned to stretch her arms and inhale life into her lungs.

In a strange twist of fate, an eremite and long forgotten, distant uncle, who rented out the little white cottage following the death of Anwyn's parents, had also passed on. The house was left to Anwyn. So she decided to sell the big London house in the heart of the city and move to sleepy West Wales. Money was not an issue. Both Anwyn and Michael had saved up a great deal from their generous salaries, while their pensions were also far from modest. The money had piled up high in the bank account with no real prospect of being spent. Both Anwyn and Michael had lived humble lives. They had never owned a microwave, a toaster or an electric kettle – a large wood-burning stove and whistling kettle had always sufficed. They had managed to live without a TV, video or a computer, preferring to fill their lives, for the most part, with the written word. Cheap second-hand books from the nearby market and Covent Garden were read from cover to cover, shared and then, sometimes sold back to the market. Their only extravagance was a small transistor radio, which would sit in the middle of the mantelpiece. They would turn it on twice a day to listen. First, to the classical music station while having dinner, and second to the long-running poetry programme which featured readings of verses throughout the ages.

Anwyn reached into her handbag and dug out a large iron key which she guided carefully into the keyhole on the plain white door. With a stiff and uncertain turn, the latch finally relented and the heavy wooden door swung open. A light switch just inside was flicked on and a single light-bulb illuminated the house instantly.

It was so much smaller than she had remembered. As a child it had seemed huge, but the world seemed bigger then. The house consisted of a communal area, with a small lounge and a kitchen space, one pocket-sized bedroom and a bathroom.

Anwyn stepped inside and wandered in a daze across the wooden floorboards. Split-second memories wandered in and out of her mind; recollections of her mother pouring gravy over a Sunday lunch, reminiscences of her father reading to her by the fireplace while she sat at his feet as he rested in his armchair, and visions of New Year celebrations, with friends and family all squeezed into the humble little home.

Byron scurried around the room, sniffing and whiffing each and every corner, his tail wagging constantly. The walls were blank canvases except for a light square patch where a picture once hung and a cross where a crucifix resided. There were no curtains, no carpets, no rugs and no furniture, bar a threadbare armchair which looked out of the bay window. The only other object in the room rested against the wall opposite the door and was a welcome surprise for Anwyn. It stood over three feet high and was six feet long. A beautiful walnut radiogram, complete with drinks cabinet, record player, beige cloth-covered speakers and a circular radio dial. On closer inspection, Anwyn saw that it was a 1961 Blaupunkt Arkansas Delux.

'What do we have here then?' Byron continued to scatter and clatter around the room, his claws providing a gentle percussive soundtrack as they rat-a-tat-tatted over the floorboards. 'This takes me back. Uncle Harold had one just like this.'

She wiped the surface free of dust, cobwebs and long-since-departed insects and unlatched the cocktail bar.

'I don't suppose there is still a nippy brandy in here.' The lid opened up to reveal an empty space. 'Bugger!'

She turned the radio switch on and a light illuminated the frequency dial. The hiss of static rustled away but she soon found the familiar tones of Talk-Two FM Radio and smiled. It was now ten o'clock. Just in time for Verse Nightly, her favourite show. Each night she would listen to a collection of poems read by people (some famous, some not) from all over the country.

'Good evening to all you poetry lovers,' said Katherine Mallory, in her traditional silky, lulling tones. 'We start tonight with a reading of Alfred Lord Tennyson's poem *This Year is Yours*. It is an uplifting and inspiring piece about new challenges, new horizons and it is read for us tonight by Tom Fielding from Durham.'

Anwyn turned the volume up a little and sat in the faded chair. As she listened, she was joined by Byron who quickly curled up on her lap.

> *God built and launched this year for you;*
> *Upon the bridge you stand;*
> *It's your ship, aye, your own ship,*
> *And you are in command.*
> *Just what the twelve months' trip will do*
> *Rests wholly, solely, friend, with you.*

As she listened attentively, Mr Fielding's voice faded and was replaced by the sound of her late husband. She closed her eyes and allowed the warmth of a memory to float over her. She felt the touch of Michael's rough hands running through her hair, as she lay in his arms on the rug by the fire in their London home. It was the day that Michael proposed to her over a mug of coffee and a china cup of Earl Grey. It yielded the start of a new chapter in their lives.

> *Your logbook kept from day to day*
> *My friend, what will it show?*
> *Have you on your appointed way*

Made progress, yes or no?
The log will tell, like guiding star,
The sort of captain that you are.

For weal and woe this year is yours;
Your ship is on life's sea
Your acts, as captain, must decide
Whichever it shall be;
So now in starting on your trip,
Ask god to help you sail your ship.

Anwyn opened her eyes as the presenter moved on to the next poetic performance and, for a second, she thought that Michael might still be with her. She scanned the room and quickly realised that she was, once again, alone.

The next morning, having spent a night in the less-than-comfortable armchair, she woke to the light of a bright new day streaming through the window of her new home. The rays brought a gentle heat to her face. She yawned and rubbed her neck free of the stiffness caused by her awkward sleeping position, before making her way to the window. The house itself may not have been anything to write home about, but the view over the ocean was something to behold. She scanned the horizon from left to right and noted the rugged coastline, the waves crashing into it and in the distance, rising proudly but lonely into the morning sky, the Smalls Lighthouse.

The distant building had stood on a small piece of rock which protruded from the sea twenty miles west of Ramsey Island. Its light shone over the waters of St Brides Bay, guiding seamen for over two-hundred years. Legend has it that one of its early inhabitants went mad on the island. Anwyn, intrigued by the view, took one last look at the lighthouse before summoning Byron.

'Come on, boy,' she said, 'time for a bit of shopping.'

CKs supermarket was a short drive from the house but a million miles from the huge impersonal supermarkets of London. Many of those colossal stores would have been almost the size of St David's itself. CK's was a quaint offering, just opposite the City Inn pub. Anwyn parked her car over two disabled parking spaces and picked up Byron. She placed him in a small shopping trolley and wheeled him into the store.

Once inside she glanced at her shopping list, scribbled hurriedly on a piece of note paper, headed through to the fruit and veg section and placed a bag of apples and box of grapes into the corner of the trolley.

'You keep your nose out!' she warned Byron, who tipped his little head innocently at her.

She wandered on, carefully stacking Earl Grey tea, Garibaldi biscuits, dog food, pain-killers, milk, eggs, bread, toilet rolls and various acquisitions for her new home. As she made her way down the breakfast cereal aisle she noticed a couple of greying women, perhaps the same age as her, in huddled, secretive conversation and staring at her. Anwyn stared back at them and turned the corner of the aisle. The gossiping couple followed her and poked their heads around a tower of Sugar Puffs.

'What are you two looking at?' she snapped. 'If you want to look at something interesting why not look in the mirror? You'll see a striking resemblance to an arse, I think you'll find.'

The women looked at her incredulously and made their

escape.

'Excuse me, Madam?' came a deep official sounding voice. 'Might I have a word?'

Anwyn turned around and saw a rotund gentleman, the store manager, with rosy cheeks, standing wheezing before her. On his lapel he wore a name badge which read, somewhat predictably, *Nigel Harmason – Happy to Help!* She looked at him in disbelief as she noted an ill-chosen wig resting perilously on his head.

'What?' she replied abruptly.

'I wonder if you wouldn't mind lowering your voice a little.'

'Well if those two bony old farts would stop staring at me then I wouldn't have to...'

'Madam,' he interrupted in a vain attempt to calm the situation, 'I'm sure that Mrs Burge and Mrs Well were only...'

'They were staring at me!' snapped Anwyn. 'I don't like being stared at. Nobody likes to be stared at! Well, except you obviously.

The shop manager was taken aback and visibly flustered.

'Well... I uh... What *exactly* do you mean by that, might I ask?'

'Well anyone with a thing like that on his head must be used to people looking at them!'

'I don't know what you mean, I have...'

'Oh, pull the other one *Nigel*,' sneered Anwyn, 'that thing on your head looks as though it has scaled your back and died a slow, painful death on your head.'

'Well, I never...'

'Get over it, *Nigel*. You are bald! Live with it! Embrace it. Why all the pretence? You are no more endowed with hair on your head than I am endowed with tits like Dolly Parton!'

'M-Madam I will have to insist that you calm yourself down or I shall be f-f-forced to ask you to leave the store!'

'Look, Nigel, dear,' said a merciless Anwyn, 'if you really do want to help, as your ridiculous badge points out, perhaps you might remove yourself and your cranial carpet from my way and allow me to continue with my shopping.'

Looking on from one end of the aisle was a slim elegant woman in her thirties. Her kindly face caught Anwyn's gaze as the standoff with Nigel continued.

'Perhaps you could talk some sense into Nigel, dear.' The woman took a step back and blushed through the beginnings of a smile. 'Can I get on with my shopping now?'

As Anwyn brushed through, Nigel passed an ill-advised comment for someone with little repost to such cutting wit.

'And I am afraid that I will have to ask you to remove that dog from your trolley, Madam.'

Anwyn stopped in her tracks and turned inauspiciously to the manager, who was already regretting his words.

'Go on then!' she said in an ominous whisper.

'What do you mean?'

'Go on then,' she drew in closer, 'ask me.'

'Well… if you don't…' he hesitated, '…it is not company policy…'

'Ask me you silly old flump!'

He took in a deep breath, 'Madam, I insist that you take that dog outside.'

'Why?'

'Because it is a health and safety issue. It could carry germs.'

'Carry germs!' she said, 'I can't even get the little sod to carry the newspaper for me! He's a Jack Russell, for goodness sake. He can't even get out of the trolley to cause a safety issue. And anyway you allow dogs, I saw the sign as I came in.'

'There is an exception for guide-dogs.'

'Ok then, he is my guide dog!'

'For God's sake!' sighed Nigel, 'You are not blind.'

'No, but I need guiding around this bloody maze of a supermarket! Who designed it, Stevie Wonder?'

'That dog is not a guide-dog! It is a normal domesticated mutt.'

'Yes and I wager it's a great deal easier to train than that furry monstrosity glued to your head!'

Nigel erupted, 'Right! That's it!' I've just about had enough of…'

Just as the manager was about to have Anwyn ejected from the store, the elegant woman at the end of the aisle called, 'Oh, there you are!'

Anwyn and Nigel turned and saw the slim form of beauty itself making her way toward them.

'I've been looking all over for you,' she said to Anwyn, who looked at her in a confused daze.

'Do I know you dear?'

'Yes, do you know this woman?' asked Nigel.

'Nigel, could I have a word with you please?'

The woman guided Nigel away, subtly whispering in his ear as they headed off around the to the next aisle. Anwyn remained rooted to the spot. She watched with curiosity as the two engaged in mumbled discussion. Within a minute or so the woman caught up with Anwyn.

'Are you ok?' she said in the sweetest voice.

'What was that all about?' asked Anwyn.

'Nothing, I just thought you could have used a little help.'

'I don't need any help!' Anwyn checked her attitude as she looked at the woman's face. There is, of course, an old saying that beauty is skin deep, but as Anwyn looked into the gently lulling eyes of the woman, she saw that in her case, beauty ran through to the bone, to the heart and to the soul.

'What's your name dear?'

'Maggie.' She smiled warmly. 'Maggie Ellis'

'I'm sorry dear, I don't mean to be abrupt, but I can look after myself.'

'I know, I could see that. But Nigel can be... well, he can be somewhat...' Maggie thought for a moment, desperately trying to find the most inoffensive term. 'He can be a...'

Anwyn decided that it was not the time to beat around the bush. 'Tit?'

Maggie laughed, 'Well, that is not the word I was looking for.'

'Oh, for goodness sake dear! Call a spade a spade, or in his case a tit.'

'Well, are you sure I can't help you with a few things?'

Anwyn held Maggie's hand, gave it a gentle squeeze and smiled. 'No dear, I'm fine. I only have a few things left to get – some Earl Grey, Garibaldi and some dog food – and I'll be on my way.'

Maggie looked into the trolley and saw that these had already been placed inside, next to Byron.

'Um,' mumbled Maggie, not wanting to precipitate awkwardness into the conversation, 'but I think you already have those in your trolley.'

Anwyn gazed inside the trolley and chuckled.

'Oh, so I have! Silly me, dear.' She glanced at her shopping list, 'Anyway, I'd best be on my way, I have a lot to do.'

'Well, it was nice meeting you,' said Maggie.

'And you too dear.'

With that, Anwyn marched purposefully down the aisle into the frozen meats section.

The following morning, the little white house was cold. Anwyn woke to the feeling of a soft wet tongue sliding in and out of her nostril as she slept in the chair. She opened her eyes to see Byron bearing down on her.

'Oh, get down, you silly bugger.'

Anwyn rose and placed her old steel kettle on the gas stove while she strip-washed in the freezing cold bathroom. Her single bar of value soap was used sparingly to preserve its longevity while a modest amount of shampoo was used to clean her silver locks. She brushed her teeth in the austere little bathroom and made her way back into the kitchen for her morning beverage.

As she drank from one of only two mugs, the other belonging to Michael, she stepped into the light of the front window and surveyed the world outside. There was a host of sea birds gathering in the bay that morning. Herring Gulls, Black-Headed Gulls, Cormorants and even Choughs could be seen splitting the wind. As she watched them gliding, flapping and swooping endlessly, she saw a path zig-zagging down the hillside to a boat-launch, which protruded out into the choppy waters. Moored to it was a small fishing vessel. Anwyn looked in interest and raised a curious eyebrow to Byron.

Anwyn got dressed and placed on a warm parker coat. She called to Byron who bounced over eagerly. Then, without a thought to reality, she shouted over her shoulder.

'I'm just off out with Byron, my love...' she waited for a response. 'Michael, did you hear me? I said I'm just...'

Just then she realised that no response would come. For a brief and beautiful moment her memory had beguiled her into believing that Michael was still with her. She stopped still as the truth hit her once again. In one painful heartbeat she lost him all over again. She took in a deep breath and closed her eyes, hoping that her memory might play the same trick twice. However, when she opened her eyes once more, the world was still missing a Michael. She put on her gloves and headed outside.

The winding path down to the water's edge was negotiated with care until Anwyn stood on the boat launch, with the salty spray from the sea rising and biting her skin. The boat had seen better days. It was a twenty-seven foot long Pearson boat with an eighty horsepower diesel engine and a VHF radio. The paint was peeling off much of the woodwork in hundreds of curved shavings of emulsion, while much of the metalwork was caked in thick rust.

'Well, it's hardly the Queen Mary, Byron.' The dog stood up and placed his front paws on the side of the boat and sniffed inquisitively. 'I don't know why they left it to me? What do I know about boats?'

Anwyn climbed aboard carefully and made her way into the wheelhouse. The radio was unresponsive, undoubtedly due to a dead battery. She wondered how long it had been since it last took to the sea. The whole thing was in a lamentable state of disrepair.

'We could sell it, Byron,' she said, 'although looking at it now I can't imagine we would get much for it.'

As she surveyed the boat once more she was struck by a moment of profound symbolism. The boat had aged, it had seen better days – perhaps, *great* days – but as it bobbed gently up and down in the gentleness of the bay, it was clear that it had been abandoned, left to decay alone and uncared for. She too had felt the loneliness that her old age had brought since Michael's death. It was also true that many friends had abandoned her in her greatest hours of need. She often wondered if a well-meaning distant relative or kindly companion would drop by in the months after Michael's passing; they never did.

'Perhaps it just needs a little love and care, Byron.' The terrier continued his curious wander. 'Maybe we could restore it back to its former glory. It would be a shame to see it go to the scrap heap.'

As the wind rolled in off the bay and the sun peered out from behind a gathering storm cloud, Anwyn resolved to recondition the boat and called to Byron before heading back up the winding path to the house.

2
Forgetting

After a day in the town ordering paint for the new boat, Anwyn retired into her chair and looked out of the window, to the crepuscular light on the ocean's horizon. She watched as a red and white speedboat zoomed across the waves.

'We'll be doing that soon, Byron,' she chuckled to herself.

The terrier, unimpressed, opened a lazy eye and then returned to his slumber, on a brand new dog bed purchased that day.

Anwyn walked to the bathroom and placed the plug in a large free-standing bath and began to run the taps. The water rushed, the steam rose and Anwyn made her way into the kitchen to make some toast. It popped up a minute or so later, taking her by surprise. She was startled but managed to compose her wits enough to smear a thin layer of value margarine on to the bread. She wandered over to the window and looked out over the waters to the lighthouse. This was a sight that she knew she would never tire of.

She let Byron outside to relieve himself and dithered around the kitchen for a while. After hearing Byron's paws scratching at the door a couple of times, Anwyn let him in and fed him a bowl of finest, luxury dog food.

'Right, Byron,' she said, 'I'm going to run a nice bath and have myself a good, long soak.'

As she approached the bathroom she could see the steam creeping beneath the door. She was unnerved. She opened the door and saw the bath filling to the brim, the excess water escaping down the overflow hole beneath the taps. She immediately halted the flow of water. Her heart raced as she wondered how the bath had come to be full. Anwyn had *no* recollection of starting the taps. Although she had been in the bathroom barely five minutes earlier, she had no memory of entering, much less running the taps. In her confusion she wondered if there might be someone in the house with her. She looked around and tiptoed out into the living room and kitchen area, half expecting to find an unwelcome guest.

'Who's there?' she asked.

There was, of course, no reply. However, still anxious, Anwyn called out again.

'If there's somebody there…' she tried desperately to sound intimidating, but soon realized the futility in that. 'I might be old, but I can still kick you in the arse… I am armed, you know.' She reached into the cutlery draw and pulled out a less-than-threatening plastic butter knife. 'Don't let me set the dog on you. He is very well trained and could rip your throat out before you could say Barbara Woodhouse!' Byron rolled over in his bed and exposed his genitals to Anwyn. She rolled her eyes in disappointment.

'Well, I'm still armed.'

She headed nervously outside and looked for signs of movement. She began to circle the perimeter of the house and as she approached the back of the house she heard a rustling sound around the corner. She looked around for a more fitting weapon of self-defence, a spade perhaps, but there was nothing. She held the butter knife tighter and began to breathe heavily, her heart pounding to a terrified allegro. She feared that her shaking might give her away. She closed her eyes, swallowed and took one last deep breath, before pouncing around the corner.

'Ahhh!' she screamed.

With a raucous squawk and a flapping of its wings, a solitary Herring Gull pulled its beak out of a waste bin having fed heartily on scraps from last night's dinner. The bird flew away toward the ocean leaving Anwyn short of breath, relieved, yet still confused.

That morning Anwyn began work on the restoration of the boat. She began clearing away the dirt from the deck before sanding down the woodwork around the helm. Byron played blissfully around on the boat launch and the nearby path, chasing away the gulls that dared to land too close to him. Anwyn observed his frantically wagging tail, his dashes from one end of the path to the other and listened to his playful yapping, and she smiled. Without Byron she would be completely alone in the world. Although all her conversations with Byron were one-way discussions, she felt that there was a deep connection between them. Her feelings for him extended beyond that of mere owner-pet associations, she felt a true love for him. In truth, she had found a deeper and more profound friendship with Byron than with any person in her life, bar Michael. At some point friends had, one by one, let Anwyn down, particularly in the weeks and months after Michael's death. They stopped calling round, the phone calls became less frequent and even the postman had started to deliver less and less post. Byron, on the other hand, was a constant source of companionship for her. During her deepest grief in the early stages he seemed to snuggle in closer to her at night, he seemed to offer more wet kisses and rarely, if ever, left her side.

'Daft sod!' she giggled.

Returning to the cottage later that day Anwyn, chilled by the winds which had whipped in from the west, filled the kettle and placed it on the stove. As she waited for it to boil she cleaned a few plates, wiped down the draining board and tidied the living room a little. She dusted down the curtains, fluffed the cushions and pulled down some stray cobwebs from the lightshade. Five minutes later she returned to the stove and, once again, decided to put the kettle on. With no memory of filling the kettle and placing it on the heat, she picked it up by the metal body ready to fill it from the tap. The pain was excruciating. She screamed wildly as the skin on her palms and fingers burned. She dropped the kettle, which fell to the floor, narrowly missing her legs and feet. She ran to the kitchen sink and, as the blisters began to form on her hands, began to run the cold water. She allowed the water to pour over her wounds and wept uncontrollably. She swore at the top of her voice and vented her anger at herself.

'Shit, shit, shit!' she said. 'You stupid bloody woman.'

She struggled to regulate her breathing and grimaced to

the ceiling through the intense pain. Startled by the noise, Byron cowered in the corner of the room, his tail between his legs and shaking. Anwyn made her way unsteadily to the telephone and with a burn-free knuckle, managed to dial the emergency service. She allowed the receiver to fall on the floor, knelt down and placed her head to the earpiece as she lay on the floorboards. A kindly voice answered.

'I need an ambulance!' she whimpered. 'I need an ambulance.'

The cottage hospital was empty. Having seen the triage nurse, Anwyn sat for a short moment looking at the posters in the waiting room. It was a unique way to be reminded of all of the cancers she could suffer from and how close she might be to having a stroke or heart attack! The room was filled with revolting pictures of tumor-ridden lungs bearing the bold-lettered slogan, QUIT SMOKING NOW! Ironically, she had never wanted a cigarette so much (since giving up twenty years ago) than she did while looking at the nauseating picture. With dressings on both of her hands, she stood up and wandered around the morbid pictures and rolled her eyes.

'Bloody hell!' she said to herself. 'Maybe it's best to just put me down now.'

'Mrs Jones,' said a familiar voice, 'would you like to come through?'

Anwyn looked up and saw the amiable face of Maggie smiling warmly at her.

The curtains were drawn around a sterile cubicle and Maggie helped Anwyn into a chair at the side of an equally sterile bed.

'I've only hurt my hands, my dear.' Anwyn shrugged off

the help. 'I am quite capable of sitting down.'

'Oh, of course you are, forgive me,' Maggie smiled. 'Fancy seeing you here. What have you done?'

'I had a minor altercation with my kettle. I forgot I had already put it on and picked it up.'

Maggie began to remove the dressing. Anwyn winced as the fabric tugged at her wounds as it was pulled carefully away.

'Oh, I am sorry,' said Maggie, wincing as if feeling the pain too. 'My goodness! You have been in the wars, haven't you.'

'I forgot I had put the kettle on already and picked it up. Ouch!' Maggie overlooked the fact that Anwyn had instantly repeated herself. She handled Anwyn's hands with the utmost delicacy, as she observed the extent of the injuries. 'Well, the good news is that you have some superficial dermal burns.'

'Oh, that is good. For a minute I thought I was wasting your time!'

'No, it's good in the sense that it could have been more serious. The skin could have been damaged much more extensively. I'll put some burn cream on your hands and I'll give you some paracetamol for the pain relief.'

'Okay,' sighed Anwyn. 'It won't take long will it? I have to get home to Byron. He's my dog. He's not used to being on his own.'

'Do you have someone you want us to call?' replied Maggie.

'No, it's just me.'

'No family, friends, neighbours?'

Anwyn snapped. 'I said, there's just me!'

'Okay! Okay!' Anwyn settled down a little. 'No matter,

we can get an ambulance to drop you home.'

'I don't need an ambulance, I can take a taxi.'

'It's no problem,' said Maggie.

'Ambulances are for picking sick people up,' said Anwyn proudly, 'not dropping healthy people home.'

'So, where is home, Mrs Jones?'

'My name is Anwyn.' She gave Maggie her address details.

'Oh, the little white house?' said Maggie familiarly.

'Yes,' said Anwyn.

'So you're new to St David's?'

Anwyn settled into the conversation a little as Maggie nursed her wounds.

'I used to live here when I was a child.'

'Here in the city?'

'In the same house,' said Anwyn, 'it was left to me after my husband died.'

'Oh, I am sorry.' Maggie rubbed an index finger a little too hard and Anwyn winced. 'I'm sorry.'

As Maggie applied new dressings Anwyn began to feel more at ease. She noted the tenderness and natural compassion in the nurse's demeanour, the soft, gentle, yet very cold which, of course, indicated a warm heart.

'So what brings you here, Anwyn?'

Anwyn shrugged her shoulders. 'I don't know. I think I just needed a change of location... a change of pace... a change.'

Maggie let out an infectious little giggle. 'Well, you've come to the right place. This old town sometimes feels so slow, it's like time is going backwards.'

'If only!' There followed an awkward stillness as both women searched for something to say. Maggie continued to treat Anwyn's burns with care and delicacy.

'Well, we're just about done here,' said Maggie. 'We just need to get your painkillers for you, so I'll get them now.'

'It's not going to take long is it? I have to get back to Byron. He doesn't like to be on his own for too long.'

Maggie paused for a moment. 'Yes, I um... I know, you... you have already asked me, Anwyn.'

'Oh, have I?'

'Just bear with me for a moment, Anwyn.'

Maggie left the cubicle and headed down a short white corridor to a small office. At his desk sat a small squat bearded man. He didn't take kindly to the disturbance as Maggie knocked on the door.

'Yes?' he said abruptly.

'I'm sorry to disturb you Dr Hemming but I have an elderly lady who I am concerned about in cubicle one.'

The doctor continued to file through his papers as he responded. 'What's the problem?'

'Well, she has been repeating herself a lot and the wounds on her hands were cause by her picking up a kettle she forgot that she'd already turned on.'

'And?'

'Well, it might suggest...'

'What?' interrupted Hemming 'We are all capable of forgetting things.'

'Yes, but at her age, surely it might point to dementia.'

'It might,' he admitted, 'but it might not.'

'Surely it's worth checking out though, Doctor.'

Finally, Dr Hemming looked up from his work and looked at Maggie. 'Look, don't you think I have enough on my plate here already? I'm up to my eyes in paperwork, more paperwork and duplications of paperwork. I don't have enough time to sort out home visits, extra medical assessments and God-knows what else, based on what? A hunch?' He sighed, seemingly aware of his own cynicism. 'Anyway, you know how tight budgets are these days.'

Maggie paused for a moment then, realising that Dr Hemming's mind was made up, headed out of his office. As she reached the door she turned back to the doctor, who had quickly resumed his administrative duties.

'I'm sorry, Dr Hemming,' she said, 'I don't really understand budgets, I deal with people.'

'Maggie!' called Hemming as she exited the room. 'I'm sorry. I don't mean to... all these bits of paper are turning me into a business man. But I am still a man. With each bloody form I fill in, I seem to move further away from what I am, a doctor.'

'No,' smiled Maggie, 'a human being.'

'Leave me her file and I'll see what I can do.'

Maggie left the office, pleased that Hemming had offered to help, but knew full well that Anwyn's case would go to the bottom of a very large pile on his desk. As she headed back down the corridor to Anwyn's cubicle, Maggie looked at her watch and saw that her shift was over. She picked up the medication from the pharmaceutical cupboard and returned to find Anwyn sitting proud and upright on the bed.

'Okay,' Maggie sat on the bed beside Anwyn. 'I was wondering if you would like to come to my house this evening for dinner.'

'Why?' asked a rather perplexed Anwyn

'Because,' said Maggie with a shrug of her slender shoulders.

'I don't understand.'

'My husband is cooking a stew this evening, and he always makes too much... §§§§§§§§§§§§and it would be nice to have some new company.'

There was pregnant pause. 'I'm not a charity case, you know.'

Maggie offered the softest of smiles. 'I didn't say you were.'

'You're not a Christian are you?' asked Anwyn, looking at Maggie suspiciously from the corner of her eyes.

'No, I'm a...' Maggie thought for a moment. 'I don't know what I am.'

'Well, as long as you're not one of those bloody do-gooder Christians. They get right on my tits!'

Maggie smiled and did her utmost to reign in the laugh which was bursting to escape out of her.

Having stopped off on the way to pick up an exuberant Byron, Maggie and Anwyn headed off through the narrow winding streets of St David's before arriving at The Old House. As Maggie opened the door a whiff of raw fish assaulted her sense of smell.

'Bloody hell!' said Anwyn. 'What is that smell?'

'Oh, that's just my son, Peter,' said Maggie, ignoring the old girl's lack of tact.

'Your boy smells of fish?'

Maggie laughed, 'No he collects scraps from the fishmonger to feed to a bird he has kind of rescued.'

'Oh, I see,' Anwyn pulled a quizzical face. 'Each to their own, I suppose.'

'Huw?' called Maggie as she led Anwyn and Byron through the front door. 'I'm home.'

'I'm in the kitchen,' her husband replied.

Maggie showed Anwyn through to the kitchen in the quaint little cottage on the main street.

Huw, with his short, straight brown hair fashioned into a perfect side parting, was taken aback as Maggie walked in with Anwyn and Byron.

'Huw,' said Maggie, 'this is Anwyn. She's new in the town, well, kind of.'

Huw wiped his food-stained hands on a somewhat embarrassing apron, complete with crudely drawn breasts, and shook Anwyn's hand gently. The visitor's eyes were drawn to the comedy kitchen attire. Huw removed the item and tried in vain to brush off the bright red blush which had come over him, while Maggie giggled.

'Is that yours?' asked Anwyn, pointing at the apron.

'Um… well…' he floundered, 'it was given to me by a friend. It was a joke.'

'It's certainly that, my dear!' sneered Anwyn

Maggie stepped in to alleviate the awkwardness. 'I hope you don't mind Huw, but I have invited Anwyn to join us for dinner.'

'Uh… no…' he stuttered, 'I mean yes… yes that's fine.'

Sensing his unease Anwyn spoke, 'I don't bite, dear.'

Brushing off the comment as best he could, Huw shouted upstairs, 'Peter, dinner's up.'

Maggie took Anwyn's coat and showed her to her chair at a large pine kitchen table. Anwyn placed Byron at her feet and requested some water for him. A bowl duly arrived and Byron gratefully lapped his thirst away.

'And who's this?' asked Anwyn as a lean, timid boy made his way to the table.

'Oh, this is our son Peter.' Maggie turned to the skinny boy as he nervously took his seat. 'Say hello, Peter.'

'Hi,' his timid voice almost inaudible.

'Hello, Peter,' replied Anwyn. 'I'm very pleased to meet you. How old are you?'

'Twelve.'

Huw placed the dinner on the table and sat down to join Peter, Anwyn and Maggie, who had now taken her seat, bringing with her a plate of bread. Huw lifted the lid of the pot of stew. The steam rose into the air and Maggie sighed happily.

'I'm looking forward to this,' she said.

'My goodness!' said Anwyn turning to Maggie. 'You were right about one thing - he does make a lot. What's in it?'

'Well,' said Huw, 'we've got carrots, potato, swede, parsnip, peas and onion.'

'Onion makes me fart!' said Anwyn without a second's hesitation. 'No meat?'

'Uh… no…' Maggie hid a smirk as her husband squirmed uncomfortably, 'I am a vegetarian.'

'What?'

'Huw doesn't eat meat,' said Maggie.

Anwyn paused. The silence was filled with an awkward anticipation of what the old woman might say next. Finally, she turned to Huw.

'You're not gay are you?'

Peter almost choked on a piece of bread as a laugh attempted to escape. Maggie too, chuckled under her breath while Huw's cheeks turned a conspicuous shade of red.

'No!' he replied.

Anwyn shrugged, 'Just asking.'

'Well I'm not!' said Huw defensively.

'Okay! Don't get your knickers in a twist!' A pause

ensued. 'No, your boyfriend will have trouble getting them off!'

Maggie and Peter laughed heartily this time much to the annoyance of Huw.

'I'm only playing,' she said. 'Now, tell me, what do you do?'

'What do you mean?' asked Huw from behind his sulk.

'For work, my dear.'

Huw assessed the situation for a moment to see if this was a genuine question, or simply another plot to insult him further. 'I run dolphin tours from down by the beach.'

A long empty pause, 'I didn't know dolphins went on holiday!'

Maggie and Peter held in their giggles and placed their hands over their mouths to hide their widening smiles. Huw picked up his dinner plate placed it by the sink and, quietly seething, he headed upstairs. As he disappeared the kitchen erupted to the sound of laughter.

After dinner, which proved more than a little trying for Anwyn on account of the bandages on her hands, the old lady sat down for a cup of tea by an open fire, while Peter played with Byron, tickling his tummy playfully. The dog licked and nibbled the boy's hand, who in turn, opened up a little.

'Why did you call him Byron?' asked Peter.

'My husband used to like poetry.'

'Oh, Lord Byron.'

'Yes, that's right,' she said, 'I'm glad they teach you *something* at school. Do you like poetry.'

'No, not really,' he replied unashamedly.

'Reading?'

'No.'

'What *do* you like?' asked Anwyn. 'I suppose you're into the interweb, boygames, phones and playingstations, aren't you?'

'What?' Peter looked to his Mother for help but she seemed just as confused. 'I like animals.'

'Animals?'

'I've got lots of pets,' he said. 'I collect stick insects, giant snails, I've got a hamster, a fish and a tarantula.'

'Well, you can keep that bloody thing away from me.'

'Don't you like spiders?'

'No, I certainly don't!' she stated firmly. 'Why don't you have a normal pet like a dog? Byron seems to like you.'

His head lowered a little, 'Dad won't let me have a dog.'

'But he'll let you have tarantula? Well that makes perfect sense!'

Maggie looked over to Huw, who by now was tidying the kitchen, and watched as his lips tightened. Anwyn's sarcasm had touched a nerve and Huw, clenching his jaw, was ready to pop. He was ready to retaliate when Maggie interjected.

'Anyone for tea?'

Later that night, having dropped Anwyn off at the cottage with the promise to help her first thing in the morning with breakfast, Maggie arrived home again. Huw had gone to bed early. When Maggie opened the door to the bedroom she found him reading a book. As Maggie slipped off her uniform Huw finally looked over the brim of his novel.

'Next time you decide to bring a Miss Marple lookalike home with you, do you think you might give me a little prior warning?'

'I'm sorry,' she said. 'I couldn't leave her though, not with her hands in that state. She doesn't have anyone to look after her. You heard her tonight, she kept on forgetting things. I think she has dementia. That's the reason she hurt her hands. What could I do?'

Huw was flummoxed by Maggie's question. 'I don't know, but you're not social services.'

'No, of course I'm not,' she replied, 'I'm far more effective than that.'

'I'm serious, Maggie.'

'So am I! If I had left her on her own she wouldn't have coped. All that social services would have done would be to send a snotty teenager around to make her a crappy cup of tea and some toast... if they sent anyone at all.'

Huw huffed and tightened his lips 'So we're going to have her around tomorrow as well?'

'No,' I'll go to her tomorrow.' A calm of sorts descended on the bedroom. 'Look, I know she's... she's a...'

'Pain the arse!' interrupted Huw.

'I was going to say... a little challenging.'

'That's an understatement!'

'She's just a bit eccentric, a bit quirky,' said Maggie.

'Yeah, and she bloody well hates me!'

Maggie sighed and rolled her eyes as she headed off to the en-suite bathroom.

'She doesn't hate you, that's just her way.'

'Why do we say things like that?' No reply came from the bathroom as Maggie ran the taps and flushed the toilet. This gave Huw a moment to moan out loud to himself. 'Why do we defend arseholes? I went to school with Ashley Connelly. A knob of the highest order! Tall, lanky, loved himself to pieces and he thought that everyone else loved him too. He would always try to be the life and soul of the party, try and crack jokes, be cool, always following the crowd along. You could see people roll their eyes as he came up to them. People used to fake diabetic comas and heart attacks just to avoid him! He would say and do the most stupid things and people would say, "Oh, that's just the way he is." To me, that's code for, "He's an arsehole of the highest order, run like the bloody clappers. Why doesn't someone say, "Piss off, you're getting on my tits, get lost before I twat you with a two-by-four!" An arsehole is an arsehole, that's all there is to it.'

Maggie re-entered the room after a quick wash, 'Did you say something?'

Meanwhile, in the cottage by the sea, Anwyn, still in the clothes she had been wearing all day, turned on the radio at ten o'clock and listened to the poetry show. She turned the volume up a little and retired to her chair. She rested her head and as the warm tones of the reader's voice came out of the speakers, she closed her eyes, barely noticing Byron as he leapt on to her lap. The day had been something of an embarrassment for her. For years she had had no need to rely on anyone else for anything. She always had Michael. However, as the years passed by with increasing speed, and as she began to accept that her memory was beginning to fail her, the prospect of having to depend on others was very real. However, there *was* no one. Anwyn's pride and independence were always very important to her and she was determined to fight to keep hold of one of the most defining aspects of her character.

As Byron snuggled in, Anwyn's heavy eyes closed, and

she felt her old age and loneliness more acutely than ever. How she yearned for Michael. The anger of his untimely passing rose through her blood once again, and the sadness and despair in her heart sent real physical pains through her chest. As she listened to the comforting tones of the radio presenter narrating Dylan Thomas, a tiny tear ran down her face and she felt a cool but soft hand on her fingers. Her heart began to beat a little faster as she could smell Michael's aftershave drifting through the night air. She could sense him there and soon the radio narrator's voice was replaced by the sound of her beloved husband, reciting passionately into her ear. She could feel the soft brushes of his breath on the side of her head as he spoke. There, in the cold darkness, beneath her tear, Anwyn could feel the warmth of her husband's presence all around her, like a lulling blanket. She heard the last lines of Michael's favourite, *Death Shall Have No Dominion* as Byron stretched his legs and yawned contently. She drifted off into a heavenly daze and could feel her husband oozing through her mind, then, suddenly, a rustle of static from the radio pulled her back to reality - back to a life without Michael. Just as she was beginning to feel the pain and yearning surge through her body once again, the presenter spoke.

'Now it is time to introduce you all to a very new poet,' said Mallory, 'whom I am sure we will be hearing a great deal of in the future. This is the first time we have featured a poem by Jack Newton and this is simply titled, *And Yet...*

And Yet...

When the wildest winds of the winter rattle the latches,
You bolt the heavy door and search for the matches.
You strike the strip and spark up a flame
And you are sure that somehow you heard my name.
Yet, you will not believe.

When the shining hues of autumn turn your path gold.
Your soul is young and tender, but the bones and sinews old.
You feel a breeze cut through you and shiver in the cold
And hear echoes of sweet musings you were told.
And yet, you will not believe.

In spring the birds sing sweetly from within the flowers bloom
While you are pacing circles in a dark and lonely room,
You'll feel a touch upon your shoulder and turn around to see
An empty space, a dusty place and an outline of me.
And yet you will not believe.

While the summer sun shines softly you're hiding in the shade,
Recounting a lover's promises that in earnest, were made.
Then you'll lay some flowers on my tended grave
And swear on your life you could smell my aftershave.
And yet you will not believe.

But one day you will just let go and in faith you'll make the leap.
You'll close your eyes, look for me and breathe me in deep.
And in belief you'll see me, and the sight will not deceive
For believing is seeing, and in seeing you'll believe.
*And you **will** believe.*

The poem told Anwyn exactly what she wanted to hear, at the time she most needed. It validated her feelings and her thought that her husband was near by. Jack Newton's poem seemed to reach right into her broken heart and reassemble it piece by piece. It brought a bittersweet happiness and solace to her fragile disposition.

The school bell rang at three o'clock, although according to Peter's wrist watch, it was two minutes late. The corridors became a hive of activity. This was always the worst part of the day for Peter. As he walked down the corridor, one or more of his tormentors would invariably accost him. They would stalk his every movement within the hoards of pupils and pounce un-noticed. The teachers were busy banging their heads on their desks at the end of another dispiriting day, dreading the thought of another night of marking, while the pupils were already thinking about the evening's televisual delights, social media or where to hide while smoking the cigarettes that their older siblings had purchased for them. The teachers had no time or inclination to pay attention to Peter's predicament.

Peter stood in the doorway of the science classroom. He waited until the corridors had cleared, looked left and right, but still felt uncomfortable about venturing out.

'For God's sake, Peter!' called the droning, cantankerous voice of Mr Bowman. 'Go home, will you? You can't stay here all night.' Peter hesitated. 'Well? What's the matter?'

Peter hesitated. 'Well…'

'Well, what?' snapped Mr Bowman. Peter had no response. 'Go…Home… Now!'

Peter stepped out into the corridor like a tightrope

walker stepping out on to the high-wire. He placed his bag over his shoulders and walked, face-down, along the corridor. Unfortunately, the peaceful sanctuary of the library was closed to him. The doors were locked early that day as Mrs Thornton, the librarian, had a pressing appointment at the cottage hospital to have a particularly nasty verruca treated. He knew that the "in crowd" were waiting to hurt or humiliate him somewhere beyond the school gates, so he made his way to the boys toilets. He pushed the door open and the stench of urine, which had been aimed at everything except the urinals, was overpowering. Long, snaking lines of toilet roll paper carpeted much of the floor and two of the taps were still running. The cubicle doors were smeared in graffiti referring to the assumed homosexuality of the chemistry teacher Mr Harmison, the greatest football team in the world (Manchester United unsurprisingly) and Tina Upson's phone number for anyone interested in teenage felatio. Crudely drawn pictures of penises and large-breasted women, illustrated by sex-crazed teenagers were, ironically, enough to put anyone off the idea of coitus, in all its grisly guises. The sight of the contents of the cubicles was too much for Peter to bear, so he leaned up against the wall in the comparatively clean corner of the revolting room. There he waited for twenty minutes, passing the time by reading his tatty and worn-out Penguin Guide to British Bird Eggs.

Suddenly, Peter was startled as the door flew open and the worrying sight of Adam Bargewood and Kelly Moore appeared, followed by a couple of their cowardly cronies. Peter's heart skipped a beat. He felt a shiver of fear run the length of his spine and sharp, prickling sensations seemed to stab in his armpits. The lanky Bargewood grinned, his crooked teeth protruding from narrow lips and his greasy hair falling down over an equally-greasy forehead.

'Oh, look who it is?' he snarled.

'It's nature boy!' said the portly figure of Moore, short black hair and an earing in his right ear. 'What are you doing in here, freak?'

'Nothing,' he trembled.

'Nothing?' said Bargewood. 'What you reading?

Peter stuttered'…It's…it's j-just a book.'

Bargewood slapped Peter hard over the back of the head. Peter cowered. 'I can see that you little shit! Don't try and get clever with me.'

Moore snatched the book from out of Peter's shuddering hands and threw it to Bargewood, who looked at the front cover in disgust.

'You really are a freak, aren't you, nature boy?' Bargewood stepped into Peter's space. 'If you weren't such a bloody girl you'd be hiding away in the bogs reading porno magazines, rather than this crap!'

'That's okay though,' interjected Moore. 'We'll put you on the right track. Turn you into a man.'

Moore took the book from Bargewood's hands and opened the graffiti-ridden door to one of the cubicles, then dropped the book into toilet, which was blocked with effluence, urine and huge clumps of toilet paper.

'There you go, nature boy!'

Peter was frozen to the spot. He wanted to protest, he wanted to do something, but feared painful reprisals from his tormentors. At that point the toilet door swung open and the school cleaner, a greying Morgan Jones, entered with his mop and bucket.

'What's going on?'

Moore and Bargewood said nothing. They simply wandered nonchalantly out of the room, barging past Jones on their way and offering little more than a wicked smile. Peter expelled a huge sigh of relief then placed his face in his hands.

Morgan Jones looked at Peter, 'Well?'

3
Building the Boat

Two weeks passed and each day, despite complaints from Anwyn, Maggie dropped by the cottage to see if the any help was needed. The complaints became less vociferous with each visit and a degree of trust was achieved on the part of both women. Anwyn continued to work on the boat, step by slow step through all weathers, much to Maggie's disapproval. The radio continued to spout poetry which eased the loneliness of the evenings, but her memory lapses seemed to be increasing. She could recall distant memories – playing alone on the beach as a child and stumbling upon a starfish, her first kiss with Michael and the melodic chimes of the grandfather clock in the corridor of her grandmother's house – but her immediate memory kept faltering. She feared that she might soon forget what Michael looked like or, just as painful, who she was.

Anwyn had arranged an appointment at the local health centre to discuss her concerns and she planned to drive into St David's early so that she could buy some groceries. However, having forgotten to turn off the headlights on her Morris Minor, a flat battery meant that the car was completely out of commission. She walked to the top of the coastal path to the main road where she sat on a bench at the bus stop with Byron. The wind from the sea swept up from the cliffside and chilled her to the bones. She fastened her coat tightly, pulled the collar up to her chin and shivered.

'Oh, Byron it's bitter isn't it?' she rubbed her arms quickly to try to create some heat. She patted her lap and invited the dog up. 'Come on, let's try and share a little heat, shall we?'

The little dog shivered and trembled. He snuggled in to Anwyn who planted a loving kiss on his brown and black, patched head. Anwyn gazed along the length of the wooden bench and observed the graffiti carved, tipex-ed, biro-ed and permanent-marker-penned along the panels.

'Isn't that awful, Byron?' The dog continued to shake. 'Bloody kids! Don't they have anything better to do? The little sods can't even spell. Give them a pen and paper and they'll write bugger all, give them a bench and you can't stop them. Perhaps schools should issue benches to kids rather than exercise books. I'd like to see the little sods dragging a bench to school in the morning. Might get them fit too. You should see the children come out of the local primary school, Byron. Christ, some of those young boys have got bigger tits than me! Thank goodness we don't live on a fault-line, the rumble that comes out of the school at home-time could trigger an earthquake of biblical proportions.'

After a little while the bus arrived. The bus driver looked at Byron, and knowing full well that dogs were not permitted, smiled and winked at Anwyn. She picked up the pooch under her arms and thanked the driver for his kindness.

As the bus meandered along the rugged, yet picturesque shoreline, Anwyn felt a kind of sensory freedom that she had only just noticed. For so many years her world had been overshadowed by skyscrapers that denied her a full day of sunshine. Indeed in the winter, the sun could barely rise above the height of the ubiquitous columns of dull, grey protrusions of stone and glass. Now all around her was space. As the only person on the bus she also noted the quiet. Back in London, commutes would consist of the intolerable tinny rattles of headphones blasting the wax out of a student's ears, the innate chatter of people with nothing better to do than moan about the unpredictable British weather, or the sound of people destroying the English language. Nothing irked her more than to listen to people who were old enough to know better, using the word *like* instead of using *said* or *thought*. She would hear, *I was like, 'yeah!' and he was like, 'no'...* and it would pain her to the core. It was as though a musician was listening to a beautiful melody played out of tune. One of the reasons she loved Michael so much was that he could transform the English language into a verbal symphony on any subject. Words dripped from his lips like the sweetest honey and Anwyn believed that when she was kissing him she could taste his language on her tongue. The air around the coast was free from the smog and fumes that she would inhale into her lungs day after day. She felt as though her senses had been cleansed.

As the bus pulled into the town, Anwyn saw the familiar figure of Peter, his school blazer smothering his meagre body, coming out of the fishmongers with a white plastic bag filled, no doubt, with fishy scraps for his sick gull. She watched him for a moment and saw in his pale face, a loneliness which she understood only too well. She saw it in the way he walked too; his head lowered for fear of catching someone's eye, his arms folded, shoulders raised up to his ears and his feet moving in tiny footsteps, as if over-cautiously concerned that he might fall at any moment. He seemed delicate, as though a single unkind word could send him to his knees.

Anwyn's experience at the doctor's surgery was a predictably miserable affair. Having secured Byron to a bicycle stand outside, a little mole-faced woman with thick-rimmed glasses and no chin, checked her in hurriedly. Anwyn sat and waited patiently and stared at yet more inauspicious posters. She sat listening to an octogenarian hacking up great lumps of phlegm, a child having a tantrum, a baby screaming and the constant ringing of the receptionist's telephone. So much for the peace and quiet. Finally, the tinny voice of the doctor called through the waiting room speaker requesting Anwyn's presence in room two.

Anwyn entered the doctor's room and saw a young man sporting a well-groomed beard stood waiting to welcome her.

'Mrs Jones,' he said cheerily, 'I'm Doctor Gabriel. It's nice to meet you, what can I do for you?'

'Um, well it's probably nothing.'

'Well, I'm sure you're right, but why don't you let me allay your concerns.'

Anwyn looked down at her hands which were beginning to gnarl with the onset of arthritis. She could cope with the physical pain of aching joints, but the thought of losing her mind was far more worrying.

'It's my memory,' she said.

'I see.'

'I keep forgetting things.'

Dr Gabriel tried to reassure Anwyn. 'Well, we all do that.'

'Yes, but I seem to be forgetting more and more. It's my short-term memory. It's not right. It's not normal.'

'Can you give me an example?' asked Dr Gabriel.

'Well, it's not just a case of occasionally going into a room and forgetting what I went in for, I mean, I was doing that when I was in my twenties,' Gabriel smiled warmly, 'this is happening every day. I flooded the bathroom last week. I started running the taps and left them running. It was only when I passed the bathroom and saw the water creeping beneath the door that I realised the place was flooded. And yet, I had absolutely no recollection of even running the bath. Some days are worse than others.'

'Okay, there may be a number of reasons for this temporary amnesia and therefore a number of possible treatments. The most important thing to realise is that...'

'...It's Alzheimer's,' interrupted Anwyn, 'isn't it?'

Dr Gabriel was taken aback by his patient's directness. He sighed and sat back in his chair. He could see that Anwyn was a wily soul who would accept nothing less than the truth, no matter how cruel it might be.

'Okay,' he said, 'it's possible. At your age it *is* possible.'

'I knew it,' said Anwyn, jumping the gun.

'*However*, it is also possible that it is something else. Let's not be hasty. We will need to undertake tests and I would like to refer you to the hospital.'

Anwyn looked at her hands again, 'Doctor Gabriel, I can't lose my memories. I have nothing else. My memory is all I have left of my husband. It *is* my husband. I can't lose it. I can't lose him, not again.'

'I understand,' said Gabriel.

'If it is dementia, what can you do?'

Gabriel shuffled uneasily in his chair. 'Well, we could try cholinesterase inhibitors."

'What?'

'They're drugs you can take and they can help control the symptoms of mild or moderate Alzheimer's.'

'But what if it's not mild or moderate?' asked Anwyn.

'Let's discuss that matter when or if it arises, shall we?' Anwyn nodded. 'In the meantime, is there anyone who can help, at home?'

'No, it's just me and Byron.'

'Byron?'

'My dog.'

Gabriel lightened the atmosphere with a kindly smile. 'No, I mean family.'

'No, there's no one.'

'I could look into some home help for you, if you like?'

'No,' she answered swiftly, 'that won't be necessary.'

'It might help you Mrs Jones, to have someone to…'

Anwyn stepped in once again, 'I said no carers. You take care of my memory, I'll take care of the rest.'

That night, as the moon fought to find a place within the gathering clouds, Anwyn treated herself to a cup of hot chocolate. She placed the milk into a small saucepan and placed it on the stove. As the bubbles started to gather on the surface of the milk she wandered over to the radiogram and turned it on in time for the evening poetry programme. She listened for a while to some Siegfried Sassoon, whose *Base Details* was read by a voice who over-performed the piece much to her annoyance. Michael would not have approved either. He hated the poets who performed the poems as if they were Shakespearian actors. He used to tell Anwyn that if they had to *act* and *project* the poem, then they had little confidence or understanding of the words; and the words were everything. She listened to the poems by Donne and Shelley and although she enjoyed them, to some extent she allowed the over-familiar words to wash over her.

Finally, the presenter, the genial Katherine Mallory, caught her attention, though for no particular reason.

'Now we turn to a particular favourite of mine,' she said, 'a poet with great heart and directness. Jack Newton, is one of our less-well-known poets but as you will hear now in a piece called, *Understanding Memories*, he has a gift for connecting to those who need to hear.'

Anwyn, having forgotten to take the milk off the stove, quickly removed the over-bubbling pan off the heat and listened to the poem, as read by the gravelly voice of Arthur Thomas.

Understanding Memories

Some memories linger,
Some come and go.
Some last a lifetime,
And some you can't hold.

You might rightly ask
Why you should recall
The sound of footsteps
Echoing through a hall,

Yet there's no room
In your mind to rejoice
In a sweet memory
Of a lost lover's voice.

You can't pick or choose
The things you remember -
Which nephew's birthday
Is the fifth of December?

But the memories that matter,
They are all made clear
With ashes to ashes,
When the next world is near.

Anwyn was transfixed. The words spoke to her as if they were intended for nobody else. The promise that all memories would be returned to the mind as one moved from life to death gave her great comfort and solace. The gentle piano music, a section from a Chopin prelude, played the show to a close and Anwyn turned off the radiogram. She called to Byron who came to her side as she headed off to bed with a hot chocolate, and meditated on the concept of the return of lost memories.

Following the early Monday morning rush of dozens of greying, frail, old folk arriving at the post office to collect their pensions, things began to calm down a little. By the time Maggie joined the queue at eleven o'clock during a break from work, the only people between her and the friendly post office staff were Mr Edgecombe from the Royal Legion and the talkative Mrs Ainsely. The latter pontificated for an age about the role of town planners and their quest for power and importance, at the expense of common sense. The young girl behind the counter was accommodating to a fault. She could see that Maggie was waiting to deliver a parcel and tried to conclude the conversation with a final line such as, 'Anyway...' and 'Oh well, never mind...' but Mrs Ainsely wasn't taking the hint. Maggie, who was in no particular hurry, found the whole situation amusing. Finally, the penny dropped and Mrs Ainsely turned to see Maggie waiting patiently.

'Oh, I do beg your pardon, my dear,' she said.

'It's okay.'

'And here I am gossiping and talking ten to the dozen.'

Mrs Ainsely finally disappeared and Maggie chuckled with the young girl behind the counter. They made a little small talk as Maggie placed her parcel on the scales to determine its cost to post recorded delivery to Cardiff. Having paid for her postage, Maggie offered the young girl a neighbourly smile, said her goodbyes and headed for the front door. As she did so, Emma entered. The attractive thirty-something, whose beauty, like Maggie's, also radiated from within, worked with Huw on the Dolphin boat tours. Yet the tension between the two was palpable. The two stared at each other for a while, considering what to say, how to say it or if to speak at all. Maggie's face was uncharacteristically stony. She tried to disguise an expression of anger which was emerging from beneath her loveliness, while Emma tried to offer a half-smile which she instantly knew would not be reciprocated. She looked down to the floor before returning her gaze to Maggie and speaking.

'Maggie,' she said, 'can we please talk?'

A thorny pause created further awkwardness between the two. 'I have *nothing* to say to you,' said Maggie. 'Nothing!'

Maggie walked out of the post office, leaving Emma standing alone, but for the uneasy girl behind the counter, who had witnessed her humiliation. Emma stopped for a moment. It was now impossible to be served by the girl, the embarrassment was too acute.

'I'll… I'll try and come back later,' she said to the girl, before walking out into the street with her head hung low, consolidating her humiliation by walking into a passer-by.

Cormorants had gathered on the rocks around the bay, extending their wings to dry their feathers in the morning sun. Anwyn stood at the window with a mug of hot tea, surveying the wonder of the world before her, yet it still couldn't fill the void in her life. How, she wondered, does one grieve? In the weeks after Michael's death she had spent most of her time sorting out her husband's affairs, then the house had to be sold, while bank details needed to be altered and a host of other trivial matters called for her attention. It all interfered with the grieving process. Tears had fallen, but not in the volume which she had expected. Her heart was broken, yet she felt that she had not cried enough. Her love for Michael suggested that she might have cried an ocean. So why, she wondered, were her eyes so dry? Where was the breakdown? Where was the uncontrollable outward show of emotion? Despite a little tear here and there, all she felt was numbness and a simmering anger.

After breakfast Anwyn and Byron made their way down to the boat launch. The paintwork was coming along nicely. In patches the boat was beginning to at least *look* as though it might be seaworthy again. As ever Byron sniffed around the rocks close by and Anwyn continued to paint. As the sun disappeared briefly behind merging grey clouds, she saw a boat approaching. It was a large white speedboat with a couple of rows of empty seats. The single occupant, wrapped up safe and warm in a luminous orange jacket, seemed familiar. As the boat neared Anwyn saw the wind-bitten face of Huw coming toward her.

'Good morning!' he shouted.

'Morning,' replied Anwyn.

'How's it going?'

'Fine, thank you.' Anwyn continued painting as the speedboat pulled up close by and bobbed up and down in the sheltered waters. 'What are you doing here?'

'I came past earlier, on a dolphin watch, with a couple of French tourists who demanded their money back because they didn't see anything. I saw you from a distance working here and I thought I'd see if you needed any help.'

'No thank you, I'm quite capable,' said Anwyn sharply.

'I know you are,' replied Huw, 'I can see that.'

There was an awkward moment of silence. 'I don't need any help.'

'You don't like me,' said Huw.

'I don't know you.'

'That shouldn't matter.'

'Look, I'm sorry if I appear abrupt, dear,' she said,

lowering her defence a little, 'but that's my manner. I call a spade a spade.'

'And a vegetarian a gay.' Huw gave a crafty smile and cheeky wink.

Anwyn looked sheepish and then chuckled a little. 'I was joking.'

'I know,' said Huw, 'and I'm sorry I was so miserable. That's become *my* manner recently.'

'What do you mean?'

'Oh,' he sighed, 'family stuff.'

'I thought as much,' said Anwyn.

'What do you mean?'

There was a long pause. Huw and Anwyn stared at each other, sizing the other up, looking for signs of dishonesty, before finally concluding that they were, if not friends, certainly no threat to each other.

'Would you like a cuppa?' asked Huw. 'I have a full flask of tea. I won't get through it all by myself.'

Huw moored his boat next to Anwyn's before stepping aboard her vessel.

'Good grief!' said Huw, as he made his way on to the boat, catching his coat on a protruding nail. 'This boat has certainly seen better days.'

'Haven't we all?' replied Anwyn

'I suppose so. How is the engine looking?'

'The engine?'

'Yes, what state is it in?'

'Well, I don't know,' said Anwyn, 'I've been rather concentrating on the exterior.'

'Do want me to have a look?' asked Huw.

'It's quite alright. I'm sure you've got better things to do than to look at a greasy old engine.'

Huw smirked 'That sounds like the filthiest euphemism, I have ever heard.'

'Oh, go on with you!'

'Honestly, I don't mind,' said Huw, pouring the steaming hot tea into a couple of plastic cups, 'I like engines. They're logical, unlike people.'

Anwyn thanked Huw for the tea and wrapped her hands around the warming cup. She took a large sip and let out a satisfied sigh.

'When you say people, do you mean your wife?'

'I mean people. I'm not the most sociable person.'

'But you were referring to your wife.'

'Was I?' asked Huw 'How can you tell.'

'I could tell something was wrong when I came to dinner. Talk about an elephant in the room. There was an atmosphere.'

'An atmosphere?'

'Yes,' said Anwyn, 'an awkwardness between you all.'

'Go on.'

Anwyn slurped down some more tea. 'You seem like… it's as if… To me, it seems like there is a great deal of love in your house. It's like it circles all around each room, I felt it in the kitchen, I felt it in the living room, but nobody seems to be taking hold of it. It's like you're all frightened of each other. Maybe you think the love won't be real. Perhaps love has let you down in the past. I don't know.'

Huw listened intently. He sat motionless and free from expression as Anwyn spoke. Anwyn took another swig of tea.

'Of course, I could be wrong!' she giggled. 'That's just the way I see things. I observe things, I analyse them. Sometimes I look too much. That's Michael's influence coming out, I suppose.'

'Michael?'

'My husband,' she said. 'He died a while ago.'

'Oh, I'm sorry.'

'He was a poet and poetry lecturer.'

'Wow! Sounds very grand. In Wales?' asked Huw.

'In London.' She smiled as a memory drifted over her like a warm breeze. 'He used to say don't just see the world; *look* at it. Don't just hear the birds in the trees; *listen* to them. Don't just touch your lover, *feel* your lover. Take your time over life. I used to want to do everything and was so busy rushing around in my life trying to achieve everything, that I didn't get time to enjoy all the things I achieved. If that makes any sense at all.'

Huw smiled. 'It makes perfect sense.'

'So, when I came to your house for dinner, I noticed lots of little things which built a big picture of what was happening.'

Huw was intrigued. 'What things?'

'Well,' said Anwyn taking a final slurp of her tea, 'on the mantelpiece there were lots of romantic pictures of you and Maggie in various embraces, they looked like ads for an old black and white movie. You both played with your wedding rings at the dinner table, rubbing them with a thumb or twisting them around. They were like a comfort blanket. There was a personalised mug on the sink waiting to be washed. It read...'

Huw interjected. '... *To the smartest wife in the world. A qualified nurse! I'm so proud of you.*'

'And yet you barely looked at each other at the dinner table. There is love there, but something's not right.'

'You're a real little Miss Marple, aren't you?' Anwyn

looked at Huw as if waiting for confirmation that her assumptions were correct. Huw took a deep breath and drank his tea in a series of large gulps. 'Let's have a look at this engine, shall we?'

Huw made his way to the engine room, leaving Anwyn on deck, and ruminated on the things she had said.

As the storm swept across the beach in sheets of fine horizontal rain, a slim figure battled the elements head-on. Peter staggered across the sand, over the pebbles and rocks, with the hood of his dull-green raincoat pulled tightly over his head. Occasionally he would slip on the seaweed which draped itself over the rocks, but still he continued. Beneath darkening skies he made his way up the beach to the cliff face. Set deep within the flaking wall was a narrow opening, perhaps a yard or so wide. Peter made his way into the darkness of the cave and removed his hood. He took a torch from his pocket and illuminated the cave walls. There, in the meagre light at far end of the cave, was an upturned shopping trolley. Inside the trolley was a Puffin, fussing and flapping excitedly as Peter approached. From out of the inside pocket in his coat he produced a white carrier bag and opened it, recoiling as the smell of its contents hit his nose.

'This stuff stinks!' he said, taking out a piece fish and placing it through the bars of the makeshift cage, straight into the gaping mouth of the grateful bird. 'What's wrong with carrots? Couldn't we compromise? I could bring a tin of tuna if you like! Either way, we'll soon have you right, Darwin.'

Peter continued to feed Darwin as the wind and rain continued to batter the world outside. From another pocket in his coat he pulled out a couple of large lumps of tightly bundled hay. They were held together with a long length of string, which Peter cut with a pen-knife. He separated the hay and, after removing the previous days dirty bedding, placed it in the corner of the trolley, making a warm bed for the bird to rest.

'Let's have a look at that leg of yours.' He picked the bird up and gently removed him from the trolley. With tenderness and care he examined the little bird's leg. 'It's getting better. You'll soon be on your way. Soon be back out there.' Peter paused. 'Can I come with you?'

Peter held Darwin with all the love he had, before planting a soft kiss on the bird's head. He stroked his perfectly white breast feathers and then ran his index finger softly down the coal black plumage on his back.

'I'd really like to come with you,' he said gently tapping the bird's yellow, orange and black beak. 'I like fish. I could survive on fish for the rest of my life. Anything to get away from vegetable stew! I should be in maths now. They're probably doing more algebra, adding letters together to get numbers. What's the point? When am I going to need algebra? I asked Dad for some help with algebra the other day. He said he couldn't help. He said that *he* had never ever used algebra. At least he said *something* to me I suppose – it's a start. Mum was too busy writing her thesis. The amount of time she spends writing I think she'll be cleverer than you Darwin. I don't even know what she's studying. I hate school. I don't know if I am going back.' He placed Darwin back in the cage, rolled up his coat sleeve and observed a large bruise on his arm. 'It's got bigger. I don't know why they do it, Darwin. Why me? What did I ever do to them? It's the same every day. You get to school and you have to find somewhere to hide. Just when you think you are safe, they find you, Kelly Moore and Adam Bargewood and their gang, hanging around like a pack of wolves.' He swallowed as he held back a tear. 'The best part of the day is after the last punch. After they have finished hitting and punching, when *they've* had enough, when they're bored, you know they'll leave you alone... for a while. I wish they were dead. I wish something horrible would happen to them, a car crash, cancer, something horrible. But it won't.'

Darwin hopped around on the trolley and began to organise the hay into a makeshift bed, his little head moving in quirky jerking movements.

'Can I stay here with you tonight, Darwin? Would you mind? I don't want to go home.'

Huw had spent a good two hours helping Anwyn with her boat and after a long day, tiredness had started to set in, although sleep was not so easy. In the darkness of the bedroom, in the stillness of the night, Huw and Maggie lay on their backs looking at the ceiling. Occasionally, a car would pass outside, its headlights casting moving shadows around the room. The light would illuminate Maggie's pale face, but Huw could not bring himself to look at her. They were in the same bed, but in different worlds. Huw could hear each and every gentle in and out of Maggie's breath. It was a lovely, gentle sound which he had always loved, but he yearned to hear her voice. He wanted to hear her talk softly, he wanted to hear her pleasured sighs during their most intimate moments and he wanted, more than anything else, to hear her laugh once again. Laughter had been in short supply in recent months.

Maggie closed her eyes and pretended to be asleep, but

she was fooling neither herself nor her husband. In a strange irony she feared what she wanted most; to be touched by her husband. She could sense his sexual desperation, she understood how acutely he needed her body and wanted nothing more than to oblige, for she had missed feeling his warmth inside her. However, some things cannot be simply brushed beneath the carpet, some words cannot be unsaid and deeds cannot be undone.

Both parties wanted to talk to each other, but neither could work out how to initiate a discussion that would not result in more crossed words. Trivial conversation would be meaningless, but profundities would weigh down too heavily on them both. In the place where they should both feel most at home, they both felt a million miles from each other. Eventually, Maggie turned her back on her husband, so that she could open her eyes. Huw turned the other way and sighed.

4
Slides

As the wind howled outside the cottage, Anwyn opened her bedroom door and fumbled for the light switch in the darkness. It was five-past midnight and after a night sitting reading in the living room, she had resolved to go to bed. However, when she finally flicked the switch, nothing happened.

'Rats!' she said.

She fumbled her way to the bedroom, her palms dragging along the walls until they came upon a doorway. Her hands were stretched out in front of her in the darkness, as she negotiated her way to the bed and was able to find a torch in the bedside table. As she lit the torch, it slipped from her fingers and landed on the floor with a thud. On retrieving it she noticed that the torch was illuminating a small cardboard box beneath the bed. She pulled the box out and placed it on her bed. With the torch held in place beneath her chin and chest, she ripped off the postal tape and unfolded the cardboard flaps. Inside were number of small plastic boxes containing thirty-five millimetre slides and reels of cinefilm negatives.

'Oh, look Byron.' The little terrier ambled into the bedroom from the living room and sat at her side on the bed. Anwyn shone the light on the slides. 'These are from our wedding day. My God! Look at me. Not quite so many wrinkles on that face, not so many lines… not so many years. At least I kept my figure, Byron. I might not have my face, but I do have my figure. And just look at Michael. So handsome.'

Anwyn ran her fingers through her hair as Byron drifted off into a contented sleep. Soon he was twitching and ticking as he began to dream. Anwyn made her way through all of the slides before pausing on the final picture, a shot of her with Michael taken on their first wedding anniversary.

'So long ago. It's like looking at someone else's life, somebody that you *kind* of know, like an old friend that you'd always meant to keep in touch with. But then thirty or so years pass by, and you drift apart and then… you forget. You forget them, you forget the things that made you friends, made you lovers, made you soul mates.'

She nudged Byron who was startled out of the sweetness of his reverie.

'Wake up Byron!' She picked him up in her arms and hugged him like a child. 'I'm frightened, Byron. I'm so scared. I'm scared of losing my mind. My memories are all I have. Michael and I never spent money on *things*. We saved it all so that we could spend it on making memories – trips to Europe, weekends in the Lake District, nights at the theatre. If I lose my memory, what will it have all been for? I might as well have bought that souvenir from the gift shop. I might as well have bought that stupid *kiss me quick* hat from Blackpool, or that little Eiffel Tower paperweight from Paris. At least I would have had something to hold on to.'

A tiny tear began to fall from her eye. It trickled through the lines in her face like the rains in Africa, making their way through the petrified riverbeds. Byron snuggled up to Anwyn and offered the simple yet loyal love and friendship that is the hallmark of woman's best friend. She closed her eyes, rested her head on the pillow and pulled Byron in closer still until she drifted into a beautiful slumber.

Her sleep pulled her into the sweetness of a memory. Her eyes opened to a late summer sun sending soft rays of gentle light through the waving branches of pine trees. She was lying with Michael on a blanket next to a picnic hamper in Shouldham Forest, Norfolk. As they stared up at the trees they watched a tiny treecreeper scurrying up the bark of the enormous pine, his little curved beak seeking out tasty invertebrates in the wood. Flitting from branch to branch just above the treecreeper was the even smaller goldcrest. It dangled precariously from a pinecone, his green, yellow and white plumage occasionally catching the sun and twinkling like a precious jewel. Anwyn and Michael watched every jerking movement of the birds as they searched for food.

'I don't think there is anything as beautiful as watching nature,' said a young Michael.

'What about watching me?' joked Anwyn.

'Well, you *are* nature?' he replied, 'so that proves my point.'

'Ooh! Nice escape!'

Michael laughed. 'Thank you, I was worried for a moment.'

'You should have been a naturalist.'

'No, thank you,' said Michael, 'I love nature far too much to be a naturalist.'

'You are so full of yourself, aren't you?' chuckled Anwyn.

'No, I mean it.' He pulled her into a close embrace. 'A naturalist spends his life measuring nature in order to understand it. Consider the ornithologist. He catches birds so that he can measure the wingspan, without marvelling over the beautiful colours. He counts the number of returning summer migrants like he's counting money, without realizing that the real wonder is that they have returned at all. He reads Darwin over and over. He spends years memorizing the Latin names of what everyone else refers to as a sparrow or a robin. All you have to do is look at it. That should be more than enough.' He ran his fingers through Anwyn's hair and cleared his throat in a faux-pretentious manner and began to recite a poem.

It doesn't need explaining
It doesn't have to make sense
There's no need for a bearded scientist
To offer his defence.

No need for academia
Or dryly written texts,
No need to know the Latin names
Of all the bugs and insects.

Never ending discussions
About why it was created -
Evolution or creation?

Endlessly debated.

You could write a paper for a journal
With lots of clever words,
That are only of any interest
To other 'learned' nerds!

All that wasted time
With your head stuck in a book,
When all you really had to do
Was to sit in the forest and… look.

'Who wrote that?' asked Anwyn with a delicate smile.

'Kitts,' he replied.

'That is *not* Keats!'

'No, Kitts.' He sat up before getting to his feet. Edward Kitts, he's in my first year composition class.

'Oh, you swine!' said Anwyn hurling a pinecone at Michael's head.

They both laughed heartily before the humour simmered down to an occasional chuckle. Soon they settled into the kind of comfortable silence that only true lovers seems to be afforded.

'But he's absolutely right,' he said finally. 'The world is beautiful, the world is cruel, there is life and death. Accept it and enjoy it. And as for you…' he leaned in closer and kissed her gently on the head, 'I don't need to understand you to know that I love you. I'm just happy knowing that I do.'

The early morning starts were always difficult for Huw, but arriving in the darkness of a winter morning was particularly trying, yet it had to be done in order to ready the boat for the day's dolphin excursions. Health and safety regulations were such that each day he and his colleague, Emma, had to examine the boat to assess its seaworthiness.

However, by the time Huw arrived at the boat launch office at seven o'clock, Emma had already put the kettle on and made Huw a steaming hot cup of coffee.

'I thought this might help you get ready,' she said uncomfortably, 'you know, wake you up, kind of thing.'

Huw took off his coat and placed it over his chair next to his desk. 'Thanks,' he said without offering any eye contact.

Emma noticed the awkwardness yet persisted. 'I could pop up to the café if you like. Get you a bacon sandwich if you want?'

'No, that's okay,' said a distant Huw.

'How about a muffin?'

'Honestly, you don't have to…'

'…I really don't mind,' interrupted Emma. 'It's not a problem.'

'I know, but I'm fine.'

Emma wouldn't relent, 'It will only take five minutes.'

'Emma!' said Huw, losing a little patience. 'I said, no. Thank you!'

Emma finally took the hint but tried not to be disheartened. She turned on the small transistor radio and tried to lighten the atmosphere with a little music. As soon as the silky tones of Crowded House's Neil Finn started singing the inappropriate, *Don't Dream it's Over*, Huw interjected.

'Can you turn that down please?' he snapped.

Emma rolled her eyes and obliged, yet she continued to try to create a lighter atmosphere. Huw booted up the computer to check the day's schedule.

'I've already checked the schedule for today,' she said. 'It looks like we have another group of Chinese tourists at nine, then this afternoon we have…'

Huw interrupted, '…I like to check things for myself. Just to be sure.'

Emma hung her head and sighed. She sat down in her revolving office chair and turned her back on Huw. Staring out of the window for a few moments, watching the waves lapping over the rocks around the boat launch, she wondered if she could say anything right at all. She shook her head before turning back to Huw.

'How long is this going to last?'

Knowing full well what she meant he asked, 'How long is *what* going to last?'

'You know damn well, what!' Emma's voice was quick to anger. 'There's only so long you can shut me out. I get it! It was a mistake!' She picked up her coffee and headed outside. 'But it wasn't just *my* mistake.'

'Where are you going?' asked Huw.

Emma flung her coat over her shoulder, and as she stepped out into the bitter morning, turned back to Huw. 'In most respects, Huw, I'm going absolutely nowhere.'

'Emma,' called Huw, 'I'm sorry. I didn't mean to…'

She had gone. Huw cursed his childishness. He knew that someone like Emma, so dedicated, so kind and so loyal, did not deserve such a lack of courtesy. He took a swig of his coffee, swore under his breath and watched as Emma diligently began to carry out the daily checks on the boat. It was an inauspicious start to a long day ahead.

The following morning the rain lashed down on the little cottage with such ferocity that Anwyn could barely hear the sound of a hard pounding on the front door. Instead she lay perfectly still in her bed and tried to hold on to the images, the sounds, the smells and the feeling of the vivid dream she had experienced during the previous night. However, just above the din of the slate roof being pelted with mammoth raindrops, she finally heard the sound of Byron barking at the front door. She stepped gingerly out of bed, slipped into her slippers and placed on her dressing gown. She opened the front door to see a sodden Huw standing in the rain.

'Goodness, you poor sod!' she exclaimed. 'Look at the state of you. Come in'

'Thanks.'

'Go and sit by the fire, I'll get it going.'

'Oh, don't go to any trouble. It's just a bit of rain.'

'A bit?' she laughed softly. 'It looks like all of it to me.'

Huw took his coat off and placed it by the front door, not wishing to bring any more water into the house. He ran his fingers through his hair and dried the rain by wiping his hands on his jumper.

'I'm sorry,' he said, 'I didn't realise you were still in bed.'

'Oh, it's okay,' replied Anwyn. 'I was just being a bit lazy. I just wasn't in the mood to greet the day just yet.'

'Why not?'

'Oh, I was thinking about the past. I was happy there.' She smiled, yet sighed at the same time. 'It's this present thingy that I don't seem to get on with. And as for the future, well that can bugger off as far as I am concerned. I would rather like to live my life in reverse.'

'Wouldn't we all?'

Huw offered to help with the tea but the Anwyn's independence was having none of it. In the meantime, Huw got the fire going. After a few minutes she came into the living area with two cups of tea shaking and shuddering in her bony hands. Huw took the beverage gratefully and Anwyn sat down in her chair. Byron curled up with Huw by the gently emerging flames.

'What brings you here?' she asked.

'I don't know.'

'What do you mean?'

'I mean…' he hesitated and chuckled to himself. 'I have absolutely no idea why I am here.'

'There must be some reason for you arriving on my doorstep in this God-awful weather.'

'I just had to get out,' said Huw

'If they catch you walking in this weather, they would never *let* you out - not even for clean underwear. They'd stick you in a padded cell with just yourself and your thoughts!' Huw laughed then took a moment to gather himself together. 'So,' said Anwyn in the ensuing silence, 'what *is* wrong?'

'It's Maggie and me.'

'Well? Go on.'

Huw took a sip of his brew and placed the cup on the floor by the fire. He paused.

'We had a big fight, last night.'

'Oh, I see.'

'Have you ever said…' he corrected himself, '…no, *done* something that you couldn't take back, that you wish you could?'

Anwyn offered a friendly smile. 'Of course, there isn't a

man or woman alive who hasn't.'

'What did you do?' asked Huw.

'I did what everyone does.'

'And what is that?' he asked

Anwyn slurped her tea and licked her lips. 'I tortured myself, cried a lot, hated myself for a while and then learned to live with it.'

'Oh!'

'There aren't any answers on what to do with the past, and mistakes are a part of the past. Nobody *plans* to make a mistake. By the time you have made them, they've been and gone – like a thief in the night. There is nothing you can do to alter them.'

'Well that's just wonderful!'

'What did you want me to say?' replied Anwyn. 'Did you want me to tell you that there is a magic word that will take everything away?'

'I had hoped you might say something a little more positive.'

'You can't *say* anything.' She drank the last dregs of her tea down, while Huw placed another log on the fire. 'You have to do something. You have to actually *do* something to make sure the mistakes don't happen again.'

There was a long break in the conversation while Huw stared into the flames and considered Anwyn's words.

'Who was she?'

'What do you mean?' asked Huw sheepishly.

'Well, it doesn't take a genius to work it out.'

Huw lowered his head, like a little boy who had just been caught with his hand in the biscuit tin before dinner. 'Emma.'

'Go on,' she insisted.

'She was, and still is, a guide on the tour,' said Huw. 'We boat the tourists around the bay looking for dolphins. She's good at talking to the punters while I steer the boat. She's the one who gives all the facts and figures about the wildlife and all that stuff. We were always close, but just good friends. She has gone through a rather messy divorce and Maggie and I were having our own troubles and we were just there for each other. Once. That's all. One day, after a shift I dropped her off home. I walked her to the door – how chivalrous I was! She's beautiful but I had never had any feelings for her. I don't know what it was but as she placed the key in her door, I suddenly felt this… I don't know. It was like a really cold loneliness. I could feel it in my muscles, I felt it in my bones. You know the feeling you get when a cold wind goes through you, and you just can't get warm? I gave her a friendly hug, as I always did, but I wouldn't let her go. I kissed her.'

'Ah, I see,' said Anwyn. 'And I suppose Maggie found out.'

'Worse. It just happened that Peter was on his way home from school and he saw the whole thing.'

'Oh no!'

'Yes, I know.' Huw placed his head in his hands and then covered his eyes as if trying to deny the existence of the world, for at least a moment. 'I didn't know if he would tell Maggie, or if he would feel compelled to keep it secret from her. All I knew was that I couldn't leave him with what he saw. I decided to tell Maggie that evening.'

'And what did she say.'

'Say?' he sighed. 'She didn't say anything, she has hardly said anything to me since. I tried to tell her that it meant nothing, I told her that I loved her, I said I was sorry…'

'But in the end they are just words,' said Anwyn, 'they have no meaning unless they have some kind of tangible reality – actions, my boy. It's not enough to say you are sorry. You have to *be* sorry, and be able to prove it through your actions. People seem to use language so lightly these days, it's no wonder that people don't believe what others say. "Sorry" isn't a get-out-of-jail card, saying "I love you" isn't a magic phrase to get someone into bed. You can only prove you are sorry though your actions, you can only really show your love through the things that you do.'

'I suppose so,' said Huw reluctantly.

'There is no suppose about it!' She got up from her chair and picked up a picture of Michael from on top of the radiogram. She handed it to Huw.

'Was this your husband?'

She nodded. 'He was a poet and a lecturer in an English department at a university.' She let Huw examine the photo for a while then returned it. 'He wrote hundreds of poems, volumes of all kinds of verse, but he never once used the word "love". He refused to.'

'Why?' asked Huw.

'Partly because, as I have said, the word is meaningless unless it is married to actions, and partly because he hated the way we used language. He used to say, "How can someone use a word about their lover that can be used in the next breath to describe a pair of shoes?" He blamed advertisers. He hated the way they would try to convince people that they would love their new line of carpet cleaners, or that they would love the latest twelve-blade razor, or the electric shoehorn!'

Huw chuckled. 'Makes sense.'

'So it will take time,' she said. 'Love takes less than a

second to say, but hours to make – if you are doing it properly!' She winked at Huw mischievously. 'And sometimes it can take years to rebuild. Give her time.'

'I suppose so.'

Anwyn and Huw continued their tea and discussed a number of things from the state of Anwyn's boat, to the state of the British education system. Anwyn was of the opinion that children didn't have to work anymore. 'Pampered little sods,' she claimed. They talked about the future, the present, the past, their fear and failures and, in doing so, began to form an honesty and candour which would become the bedrock of a friendship. Anwyn showed Huw the slides and 8mm negatives that she had perused the night before, and asked if there was anywhere in St David's that might be able to convert them in such a way that she could see them once again and hear her husband's voice.

'I don't think you'll find anything like that here,' he said inauspiciously. 'You'll probably have to go to Swansea for that.'

'Oh, well never mind.'

'I could take it for you if you like?' said Huw.

'No, that's okay,' said Anwyn, proudly trying to mask her disappointment. 'It's nothing important.'

'Well, if you change your mind, let me know.'

The storm outside had abated and shafts of sunlight could be seen beaming through the clouds out to the west. Huw finished off his beverage which, neglected due to ongoing conversations, had gone stone cold, and left.

5
Wounds

The front door slammed. Before Maggie could greet Peter, as he entered after another nightmare day at school, he sprinted upstairs and straight into the bathroom. As he flicked the lock, Maggie called out to him.

'Peter,' she shouted, 'is everything okay?'

'Yes Mum,' he replied. 'I'll be down in a minute.'

Peter looked at his face in the bathroom mirror. He looked at the state of his unkempt hair, complete with a wandering parting, which meandered through his dark waving locks. He moved in a little closer still and noticed the red rings around his eyes from where tears had recently fallen. He placed his hands over his face, closed his eyes and tried hard to imagine a world where he would never feel such pain and loneliness. He tried to ameliorate his heavy breathing and soon it moderated to more comfortable ins and outs. He removed his hands and opened his eyes slowly hoping that he was in another world. However, when he caught sight of his reflection again he saw the same frightened, angry and lonely child.

He ran the taps and the steam from the hot water began to fog up the mirror and watched his features fade away. If only it was that easy. Gingerly, he removed his school tie and jumper and dropped them to the floor. Then, one by one, he undid the buttons on his white shirt and revealed a skeletal body covered in bruises. Some of the older bruises had faded to a light yellow hue, while the more recent marks ranged from black to purple to various shades of blue. Each mark represented an unprovoked attack from Kelly Moore and Adam Bargewood and their cowardly cronies. Peter placed his face in the sink and wondered how easy it might be to breath in. He didn't care if he would be considered a coward (people already thought worse of him) for taking his own life, he just wanted it to stop.

'Peter!' called Maggie once more. 'Are you sure you are alright?'

'Yes, Mum,' he replied as he pulled his face up out of the water, 'I'll be down now.'

Peter did not head downstairs. Instead he went to his room and closed the door behind him. He put on a long sleeved shirt so that his wounds would not be visible to his parents. He wandered over to his desk and looked inside the small glass tank to see if he still had the same number of stick insects that he had earlier that morning. All were accounted for so he went to his aquarium and dropped some fish flakes into the water and watched as the Tetras consumed them. After feeding his Syrian hamster and allowing it to wander around his room for a while in a plastic ball, he made his way to a larger glass tank and proceeded to pull out a bulky Mexican Red-Knee Tarantula.

'Hello, Terry!' he said softly. 'How are you today?'

Peter allowed the spider to crawl across his hands and up his arm. This was the one moment of happiness during his day. He smiled warmly as the arachnid wandered, step by hairy-legged step across his chest to his other arm. He ran his index finger softly over Terry's hairy abdomen and marvelled, as he did every day, at the animal's striking red and yellow markings. The friendship was simple. It was unaffected by the strange and unpredictable nuances of human relationships. The spider allowed Peter to handle him in return for safe refuge, food and water and all Peter required in return was the ability to hold him from time to time. It was the most basic of loves, but in some respects, the purest. Terry clambered up on to Peter's right hand and stopped long enough for Peter to stare into one of the spider's many eyes. A thought occurred to Peter which caused a broad smile to appear on his face.

'You couldn't do me a favour,' he said, 'could you?'

Later that evening after Peter had gone to bed, Huw and Maggie sat down at the kitchen table together and shared a pot of tea. Huw still heard Anwyn's advice in his head and was ruminating over the best way to show his love for Maggie. He was prepared to give it the time, the years that might be required, for he knew that he loved his wife, but knew that *she* needed to know that too.

'How was your day?' he asked.

Maggie was taken aback. 'I'm sorry?'

'I just wondered how your day was.'

After a long pause and a simple smile, Maggie finally responded. 'You know, I can't remember the last time you asked me that.'

Huw felt a temptation to remind his wife that he had

asked her on many occasions, only to be met by single word responses. He was also aware that it was just as long since she had asked him about his day. He paused and bit his tongue.

'Which is why I am asking you now.'

'It was okay, thanks.' Huw's expectant eyebrows asked for more information, Maggie was somewhat lost for words. 'Um… Well… I…Oh, a nice gory injury today, I thought of you.'

'Oh, thanks,' chuckled Huw.

'No, I mean I know you have a grim fascination with blood. That's why you watch the Terminator films so often.'

Another laugh. 'Oh, well that makes sense.'

'There was this guy from that building site out of town, you know, on the main road?' Huw nodded. 'He had been sitting down having his lunch below some scaffolding when a guy above him carrying some breezeblocks on his back slipped. One of the breezeblocks fell down two stories, right on to his shin bone.'

Huw winced, 'Yuk!'

'It pretty much snapped his leg in two. I was one of the first on the scene with the ambulance. What a mess!'

'I don't know how you do it,' said Huw. 'I've never understood it.'

'Well, I don't understand how you can go out on the sea everyday and not throw up every five minutes.'

Huw sighed softly and reached out and touched his wife's hand. 'I suppose there are a lot of things we don't understand about each other.' Maggie gave an affirming smile. 'But, that doesn't mean that we can't… learn again.'

Peter made his way head-down through the long corridor and wove in and out of the dozens of children making their way to morning registration at St David's High School. As he walked he did his best to ignore heckles of, "Hey, it's Nature Boy!" and much worse, and even managed to walk on after Marc Vickers had stuck a foot out to try and trip him. Peter stumbled but managed to carry on. Finally, he placed his PE kit in his locker. His was easily found within the long line of lockers as it bore various cruel and cowardly comments. Today a new obscenity had been scribed just above the lock. FREAK OF NATURE! Not particularly original, he thought, but at least it was spelled correctly. Next to his PE kit he placed his lunch box and his raincoat, before moving to the locker two rows along. He waited until the corridors had cleared and with a screwdriver, which he had liberated from his father's toolbox, forced the door open.

The lunchtime bell usually signalled the beginning of the worst part of his day, the time when Kelly Moore and Adam Bargewood would seek him out relentlessly and use him as a punch bag. However, on this day, he was looking forward to what might transpire in the dinner hall.

Peter sat down on the end of a large rectangular dinner table and watched the other children as they looked for somewhere other than near him to consume their unhealthy meals of chocolate, crisps and left-over pizza. Soon his adversaries came into the hall and sat close by. Thanks to the eagle-eyed dinnerladies, Peter knew they wouldn't try anything in the food hall, he knew he was safe from the physical abuse - *that* would follow later. However, the verbal hostilities would come right on cue.

'Well, I never!' squeaked the pathetic Bargewood, 'It's

Nature Boy!'

'How's it going freak?' added Moore.

Peter refused to engage. Instead he placed a small carrot strip in his mouth and ate with little bites.

'Hey! Nature Boy!' said Bargewood, 'what's up?'

'I don't think he understands you mate,' said Moore, deliberately talking louder to ensure that Peter heard him. 'Maybe he don't talk the same language as us. Let me try.'

Moore proceeded to run through a number of animal noises before concluding with a loud raucous seal impression.

Moore shrugged his shoulders, 'I don't know what fucking animal he is!'

'They should put freaks like that in a cage so we can learn all about it,' said Bargewood tearing the tab off his high-sugar energy drink. 'I don't even know what sex it is!'

Moore laughed uncontrollably as he pulled out his lunch box. 'Let's turn it over later. We can see if it has any bollocks – apart from that set on his fucking forehead!'

Peter continued to eat quietly and refused to give them any eye contact or respond to their cowardly taunts. However, out of the corner of his eye, he kept looking toward Moore's lunchbox.

'Hey! Peter!' said Bargewood. 'You look a little bit lonely mate. You still struggling to make friends with your own species? Well, I've got a nice dirty rat in my back yard. I'll see if I can fix up a date for you.'

'I don't know Adam,' said Kelly, 'even rats have standards, you know.'

Just then, from out of the corner of his eye, Peter watched Kelly Moore take the lid slowly off his lunchbox and reach inside. As he did so Moore let out spine-tingling, high-pitched scream, which did nothing to promote his hard-boy image.

'JESUS CHRIST!' he yelled.

There inside the lunchbox was Terry. He barely moved as Moore recoiled in horror. The tarantula slowly climbed over the top and out on to the table. Moore began to shake and cry as the spider made his way to his untouched cola can. The rest of the hall focused their attention on the teary and startled Moore.

'Oh, thanks,' said Peter in a proud and cheery voice, 'you found Terry! I was wondering where he had got to.' Peter picked up the spider and headed toward the quivering Moore. 'I think Terry would like to say thank you. I'm glad to see he had enough air in there. Just as well I pierced a few holes in the bottom of the box.'

Moore ran out of the food hall as fast as he could. 'Who would have thought? An arachnophobe!' Peter turned to Bargewood 'Perhaps you'd like to say hello to Terry?'

Bargewood took a step back. 'You're a fucking freak, Nature Boy!'

The rest of the hall drew closer to Peter to see what was causing the commotion. Far from looking on in admiration, the other pupils seemed to sneer at him. They shook their heads and mumbled yet more insults under their breaths.

'Peter Ellis!' yelled Mr Bateman, the head teacher, from the other side of the hall. 'Put that thing away and make your way to my office please.'

A soft but diluted sunlight shone on Anwyn's face as she sat in Dr Gabriel's surgery. She rubbed the aches and pains of arthritis in her knuckles, while the genial practitioner scrolled down his notes on the computer. Anwyn's calm exterior hid the butterflies in her stomach. She had been trying to think of the best way to approach the day for weeks, following the blood test she gave in the very same room. She had tried to be positive, to tell herself that everything would be fine, but felt that such an approach might tempt fate, even though she was not superstitious in the slightest. Latterly, she tried to convince herself that she had Alzheimer's, so that when Dr Gabriel finally broke the news she would have prepared herself. She tried not to think about it at all but after each memory lapse, such as leaving the hose on in the garden or forgetting to let Byron in from the yard, only realizing when she heard his cries and barks as the rain lashed down upon him, she was reminded of the reality of the situation. During the weekends, while she worked on the boat with Huw and in the evenings as she conversed with Maggie, she kept her issues to herself, although her new friends were more than aware of her memory shortcomings.

'Right, Mrs Jones,' said Gabriel, 'How have you been? Are you still having problems with your memory?'

'Yes,' she replied.

'Do you think it is getting better or worse?'

'I don't know,' she rubbed her fingers a little harder as her nerves began to take hold. 'I have good days and then I have bad days.'

'And what about today?'

'It's okay.'

'And what was it like yesterday?'

Anwyn became restless. 'Look, just tell me what the results were. Do I have Alzheimer's or not?'

Dr Gabriel sighed. 'There's no indication from the tests of any condition which should adversely affect your memory.'

'So what does that mean?'

'As I told you before Mrs Jones, there is no single test to diagnose Alzheimer's. Now, you said previously that you were not aware of anyone in your family having the condition, so that, coupled with the test results, is promising.'

'So what happens now?' she asked

Gabriel reclined in his chair. 'I'd like to refer you to a neurologist.'

'What will he do?'

'He will take an MRI scan of your brain to look for any abnormalities.'

Anwyn chuckled nervously. 'Like tumbleweed, in my case!'

'Try not to worry,' said Gabriel. 'I know it's easier said than done, but until we know more, there's no point thinking the worst.'

'Indeed it is easier said than done,' said Anwyn. 'I need my memory, I know that sounds a rather obvious statement, but I have nothing else.'

'I understand Mrs Jones, I really do.'

Anwyn stood up and looked out of the window. Gabriel, despite his busy schedule, allowed Anwyn the time to amble up and stare at the world outside. She looked up at the clouds forming in a light blue afternoon sky and tried to make shapes of them, and for a moment was taken back to a childhood memory.

'I remember lying down on my back, on the cliff top in Penarth. We were visiting friends. We had been playing on the swings, Father and I. We looked up at the sky and tried to make faces, animals or shapes out of the patterns in the clouds. Not very original, I know, but the thing is... I can't remember what we saw in the clouds, but I can remember how I felt as we looked up.'

'What was that?' asked Gabriel, putting the top on his biro and placing it neatly in his shirt pocket.

'Happiness,' she replied. 'Pure, untainted happiness. I can feel it now if I try hard. But if I lose my memory...' She became a little emotional and her voice broke as it was challenged by the onset of a tear. 'I wish I could have a clear out. Strip my mind of all the bad memories... running over a deer as it ran out into the road in Norfolk, being mugged at Waterloo station in 1973, losing Michael...'

Just then Dr Gabriel's intercom buzzed. The unsubtle voice of the receptionist informed him that his eleven o'clock meeting was waiting for him. Gabriel looked most displeased as he pressed the button to reply.

'Mrs Marcus,' he replied, 'I am fully aware of the time. Mr Bowley will have to wait until I am done.'

Anwyn could almost feel the doctor's exasperation, so she gathered her handbag and coat.

'I'm sorry,' she said, 'I have taken up too much of your time...'

Gabriel tried to halt her exit. '...No there's no rush it's just the receptionist... you see she's new and...'

'...No, honestly I'm fine,' she said 'like you said, let's just wait and see the results of the scan, shall we?'

Anwyn saw herself out of the consultation room, the receptionist almost saw herself out of a job.

6
On the Beach

The rain swept sideways across the beach, picking up surf from the sea swell in the storm. The darkening grey hues of the clouds gathered above, stretched inauspiciously along the horizon and soon all seemed black. Peter could hear the call of the oystercatchers gliding low along the waterline, occasionally stopping to look for food in the wet sand. Their bright red beaks were the only colour vibrant enough to punctuate the greyness of the world around. He pulled the zipper of his unfashionable parker coat all the way up to the hood and walked face-down so as to shield himself from the elements. He left size-five footprints in the sand, big enough to be followed.

He made his way up to the cave at the top of the beach, over the slippery seaweed and the sea-polished rocks, which led to Darwin's place of sanctuary. For the last three weeks, Peter had continued to come daily to the cave to tend to the Puffin, which finally appeared to be close to a full recovery. The bird flapped with excitement as Peter entered the cave. Even behind Darwin's melancholic black eyes there seemed to be the signs of enthusiastic anticipation within. The striking red bill seemed to illuminate the walls of the cave, as well as Peter's heart, like a roaring flame.

'Hello, my little friend,' said Peter, taking a carrier bag of fish meat from inside his coat. 'What have I got for you?' He placed the fish, scrap by scrap, into Darwin's grateful mouth. 'I think you are about ready to go, boy.' Peter sighed. 'You don't *have* to go, you know. You can come home with me if you like. I could take care of you at home. I'm good at looking after animals – I'm not very good at anything else – but I'd make sure you were safe, I'd make sure you were happy and I would... What am I saying.' He placed another scrap in the bird's beak. 'You want to go home, don't you? You want to be with your friends. I'm sorry. I just... I enjoy coming down here, talking to you. You don't judge me. You just listen – if only people could do that. Teachers, parents... nobody wants to listen, especially to Nature Boy. When I'm with you I feel safe. In here nobody can find us, no one knows where we are.' Peter took off his parker uneasily due to new bruises from Moore and Bargewood. He lifted his shirt to look at the progress of the wounds. 'They can't hurt me anymore, Darwin. They can't. They can hit me, spit on me in the playground, piss on my clothes in the changing room, stab me with pencils... they can do anything now. They can even kill me if they like. But I've won. I beat them because I have seen them as weak as I appear to them. When Kelly Moore opened his lunchbox and saw that spider crawling all over his food, when he cried like a little baby, he lost all the power he had over me. He can do what he wants now, but he knows that I saw him cry. He's no stronger than me.'

Darwin hopped around inside the shopping trolley, from corner to corner and all points in between. As he watched, Peter thought Darwin was the most perfect thing in the world; perfectly adapted to his life on the sea, perfectly adapted to its diet and perfectly suited to every notion of beauty. He loved Darwin. He knew that releasing Darwin was the right thing to do, but it was also the hardest thing to do. For weeks he had spent an hour or so each day talking to the little bird, telling it his hopes and fears with a candour he had never displayed to anyone or anything before. He had no way of knowing or proving it, of course, but he felt that Puffin was grateful to him for nursing him back to health. People were complicated, he thought, people were cruel and selfish and they represented all that was dark in nature. Darwin, hip-hopping around his little abode, *was* nature.

Peter shone his torch light on his watch to check the time and realised that he was late for tea. He gathered his things together and gave one last scrap of food to his friend.

'I'll see you tomorrow,' he said with the softest of smiles. 'Get some rest, Darwin, tomorrow you go home.'

It was still raining when he stepped out of the cave. He pulled his hood up once more and staggered out into the storm. He squinted his eyes and saw the faint sparkle of the lighthouse in the distance. Was it shining for him, he wondered? Or perhaps it was a warning. As he walked away a figure emerged from behind a large stone boulder by the entrance to the cave. When Peter was but a speck in the distance, the figure slowly entered the cave.

The next morning the sun shone gently above the calming

seas of the bay. On the rocks below Anwyn's simple abode, cormorants and shags extended their wings to absorb as much the meager heat as possible. Byron lay still in his bed, curled up warm and comfortable, occasionally twitching his nose or jerking a leg as his dreams, whatever they might have been, became more active. However, the little dog leapt into consciousness, as a firm knock rattled the front door. He yapped and barked enthusiastically, wagging his tail and turning in circles.

'Alright, Byron,' she said, opening the door, 'that'll do!'

Maggie was waiting. 'Got anything planned this morning?'

Anwyn looked confused. 'No, why?'

'Get your shoes on, we're going for a walk.'

Within half an hour or so, Maggie parked in a tiny layby off a quiet, non-descript costal lane.

'Where are we?' asked Anwyn

'We're going to Caer Bwdy Bay.'

'Why?'

'Because we are,' replied Maggie.

'There aren't going to be loads of other dogs there, are there?'

'I doubt it.'

'Good, because if Byron gets a whiff of another dog, he is likely to shag it to within an inch of its life, male or female. Randy little bugger.'

Maggie lifted out a whicker hamper from the back of the car and placed a tartan rug in Anwyn's unsuspecting arms.

'Here, hold this.' She closed the boot. 'Right, now hold my arm, some of the ground might be a bit tricky.'

Anwyn took exception. 'I don't need your arm! I can

walk by myself, you know. I might be old but I'm not dribbling into my porridge yet. I can manage to put one foot in front of the other for Christ's sake!'

'Alright!'

The two women made their way down a long, meandering coastal path, lush with the greens of early summer foliage, pierced sporadically with blossoming flowers of delicate, white sea campion and the soft yellows of cowslips. Daisies popped up here and there, as did the dandelions. The grass around was long and felicitously unkempt.

'Hardly anyone knows about this place,' said Maggie.

'Well, certainly no one with a bloody lawnmower or strimmer has come this way in a long time,' replied a moaning Anwyn.

Maggie ignored the old girl and pushed on through the path. Anwyn, eager to make a point to deny her advancing years, overtook Maggie and strode purposefully in front. As she walked she slipped in a recess in the ground and fell hard.

'Oh, bloody hell!' exclaimed Maggie. 'Are you okay?'

Anwyn picked herself up and point blank refused any assistance from Maggie to aid her to her feet. 'I can get up myself!' She wiped away the mud from her coat and rubbed the dirt off her hands, before proudly marching on. Maggie shook her head incredulously and then followed.

'Stubborn old cow!' she muttered under her breath.

Owing to her immutable determination and a firm desire to hide all weakness from Maggie, Anwyn was first to make it to the pebbled beach. Byron, who had wandered the long narrow path through the grass metropolis, emerged as though leaving a huge green tunnel into the light and the wide expanse of the stony beach. Anwyn extended her arms either side in the name of balance, as she wandered unsteadily over the pebbles to the more negotiable sands of the low tide. Maggie arrived shortly afterwards and began to unpack the hamper while Anwyn unfolded the rug and placed it on the sand. Maggie pulled out a flask and removed two plastic mugs from the top.

'Tea?'

'Yes,' said Anwyn, without the slightest consideration to tone or manners. 'It's not one of those fancy teas is it?'

Maggie kept her cool. 'You mean Earl Grey?'

'Yes, or that one that stinks like the underside of a barbecue.'

'Lapsong suschong.'

Anwyn tutted and rolled her eyes, 'Bloody puff tea!'

'I wasn't aware that a tea bag was capable of establishing a sexuality!

'Just give me a good old-fashioned cup of tea.'

'Well that's what this is!' said Maggie just losing her patience a little. 'It's not decaf, it's not low in fat, it's not high in fat, it was made from ordinary tea leaves in an ordinary factory in an ordinary town by ordinary people!'

Anwyn, for the first time in their friendship could see that she had irked the impeccably placid Maggie. She thought for a moment as Maggie poured the tea.

'They weren't poor people, were they?'

Maggie shuddered with laughter. 'Oh, shut up!'

Anwyn took a sip of tea, wrapping her hands around the mug for comfort. When friends are comfortable enough to tell one another to shut up they can also enjoy silences together, as they did for a few moments while they stared out to sea.

'I'm sorry,' said Anwyn softly.

'What for?'

'For being a miserable old bag.'

'That's okay,' replied Maggie.

'You weren't supposed to agree!' joked Anwyn.

'You never talk to me as a friend.' Anwyn looked somewhat perplexed but allowed Maggie to continue. 'You have told me a little about your past, we laugh and we joke but it's like… it's like you're hiding something. I don't mean in a deceitful way but rather… It's like you are trying to protect me from something.'

'You do read a lot into things, don't you young lady?'

'My Dad told me that life was in the detail. You *have* to look into things.'

'You've never spoken about your parents.' Anwyn gave a wry smile, 'Now whose hiding things?'

Maggie grinned sheepishly. 'He was a paper merchant. It was just the two of us. Mum left when I was a child.'

'I see,' said Anwyn.

'She suffered from severe postnatal depression. She just couldn't cope apparently. She just changed. One day she was there, the next day she was gone. I would have been about eight or nine months old. So, I never really knew her.'

'Are you angry about that?'

'How could I be?' Maggie replied. 'If she never had me, she wouldn't have become ill. What right do I have to be angry?'

'You don't know that,' said Anwyn.

After a brief moment of thought, Maggie offered the most delicate of smiles. 'No, of course, I'm just being silly. It's just a case of *what if…*'

'And your father?' asked Anwyn, keeping one eye on Byron as he ran excitedly along the beach, stopping every now and then for a good, long sniff.

'Dad was great. He and I were very close.'

'Were?' enquired Anwyn.

'Yes, he died about eighteen months ago.'

'Oh,' Anwyn bowed her head, 'I'm sorry.'

'No, it's fine.' Maggie cooled her tea with a soft blow of her lips. 'He had been ill for a while and he was almost happy at the end. It was as though he felt he had said everything that he needed to say – he told me and the rest of the family that he loved us – he'd done everything he wanted to do. He was never particularly ambitious for money or status. He was always pleased to just have me and I was just happy to be with him. After Mum disappeared he quit his job at the paper company, sold the big house, bought a little bungalow, just big enough for the two of us and started his own business as a local handyman so that he could be close to me. So at the end I had a steady job, a marriage and Peter. Dad was happy with that.'

'He sounds like a wonderful man,' said Anwyn in softening tones.

'He was. Would you like to see a picture of him?' Maggie's face lit up, like a proud child coming home from school to show off a bright new painting. She took a picture from her purse.

'He was a very handsome gentleman,' said Anwyn.

'I know.'

'So how come you ended up with the ugly mug that is your husband?'

Maggie laughed, 'Oh, he's not that bad.'

'Well he's no oil painting,' joked Anwyn, 'more of an oil

spillage really!'

As the laughter was quelled by the onset of silence, Anwyn looked at Maggie and considered how best to ask her next question. Tact was never her forte.

'So where did things go wrong?'

Maggie put her cup down and pulled her windswept hair out of her eyes. The wind was beginning to pick up so she wrapped her coat around her shoulders and brought her knees up to her chest to keep warm.

'You've been speaking to Huw.'

'He loves you,' said Anwyn.

'I don't doubt it,' replied Maggie, 'and I know he's sorry. I can even understand why he did what he did.'

'What do you mean?'

'Well, after Dad died I kind of went missing, so to speak. I wasn't easy to live with. He tried *so* hard to show me kindness, love and... Oh, I don't know. I just wasn't ready to see it; any of it. He was there, but I just wouldn't let him in. He offered so many kisses and hugs but I denied him everything.'

'Why?' asked Anwyn

'I don't know.' A shiver ran throughout Maggie's body. She shuddered. 'I wish I could explain it.'

'I suppose that's just what grief does.'

'But I hardly cried. I never broke down and...'

Anwyn interrupted. 'That's not how it works, well not in my experience. We all walk through the same shit, just wearing different shoes.'

'That's an interesting extension on Oscar Wilde!' laughed Maggie.

'What?'

'You know, "We're all in the gutter..."'

Anwyn smiled in realistaion. '…but some of us are looking up at the stars.'"

'Anyway,' said Maggie changing the subject, 'you never talk about your husband.'

'Oh well, there's not a great deal to say about… um…about…' Anwyn clicked her fingers to try to spark her memory. As she did so, she realised that she was forgetting the very thing she most yearned to remember – her husband. If she closed her eyes could she could see his face, she could hear his voice, smell his aftershave and feel his warmth, yet his name was unknown. She tried again to recall his name. Maggie gave her time to think, yet Michael's name did not come to her. Anwyn froze. Even as the strengthening wind began to blow sand into her face, she remained motionless.

'I want to go home,' she said without expression.

'Why?' asked Maggie. 'What's the matter?'

'Just take me home, please!'

Anwyn hollered at Byron who by now was chasing the incoming and outgoing wavelets and gnawing and gnashing at the bubbles riding the crests of the waves. Maggie sat still and stupefied as she watched Anwyn head back up the beach. She cut a lonely figure, walking without the purpose of her earlier steps, then disappeared up the path to the car.

7
Fury

Peter sat three seats from the end of his row in morning assembly. The hall was full of pupils yawning, coughing, blowing their noses, breaking wind to sniggers and dreading Mr Bateman's mercilessly cruel PE lesson. The principal addressed the pupils in soporific, drawn-out monotonal sentences which made heavy eyes seem even heavier. Even the teachers, sat around the perimeter of the children herded like cattle, seemed to be nodding off. To relieve his boredom, Peter tried to calculate how long, first in minutes, then in seconds, it would be until the bell rang for the end of school. Once that task had been completed he moved on to the ceiling tiles. He counted them twice to make sure that he hadn't miscounted the first time. He was about the count the window panels in the hall when the hand of Sarah Evans reached over his shoulder and passed a torn piece of paper folded in half. He read it and his heart sank. In large, capital letters it read, SHAME ABOUT THE PUFFIN NATURE BOY!

Peter looked up and around to see where it had come

from, knowing full well that it had come from Kelly Moore and Adam Bargewood. Finally, he caught sight of Moore, who grinned and waved sarcastically, while Bargewood mimed a flapping motion with his hands. He looked in their eyes and knew deep in his heart that evil had been done. Without a moments hesitation Peter leapt out of his chair, to the surprise of everyone around, and clambered over those closest to him to get to the end of the row, then sprinted down the aisle and out of the hall. He ignored the calls of the teachers to stop where he was. In fact, he barely heard them. He ran out of the school, out of the town and down to the beach without feeling the ground beneath his feet. He thought nothing of the roads or traffic, or people standing in his way, the only thought in his head was for Darwin. He feared the worst and struggled to hope for the best, knowing, as he did, the depths of cruelty that Moore and Bargewood were capable of descending to. His stomach churned, his heart raced uncontrollably and the rhythms of his blood pumping through his aching head were relentless.

By the time he had made it to the beach he had stitch pains in his stomach, which he paid no heed to as he slipped and slid over the rocks leading to Darwin's cave. As he entered the darkness of the cave he began to feel tears emerging from the corners of his eyes, his face felt hot and tingles ran through his arms and down to the tips of his fingers. Then, with a crack in his heart, he saw Darwin slumped on his back with his wings spread wide, next to the disturbed shopping trolley.

Peter picked Darwin up and cradled him in his arms. The little bird's head rolled and flopped around like an unloved rag-doll. Outside Peter could hear a storm coming.

The winds picked up and the sounds of the ocean waves thundered in from the west. This rain swept in sideways across the beach, swirling one way then another. Peter sat in the entrance of the cave with Darwin in his arms, waiting for the storm to abate. As he did so he stared at his little friend's dead body and allowed his tears to fall from his eyes, gather at the tip of his nose and drip on to Darwin's feathers. As the tears drip-dropped onto his body he rubbed them into Darwin's chest and so he thought, into his heart. The final offering of unconditional love.

'I'm sorry, boy,' said Peter through his tears, 'I'm so sorry. I should have let you go sooner. It's just that... I didn't want you to leave me. I didn't want to be alone. I was going to let you go today, honestly.' Peter's eyes surveyed Darwin's body. He couldn't tell how the bird died, but from the blood on the head he felt sure that the bird had been hit with something. All he did know was that Bargewood and Moore hard murdered his friend. 'What have they done to you, boy?'

Two emotions – grief and rage – fought for supremacy within his mind. The more he looked into the cold eyes of Darwin, the more the sadness took hold of him, and the more he thought about the violent circumstances of the puffin's death, the more the rage ran through his blood. While his eyes were open all he saw through his tears was Darwin, but with every blink, in the split-second darkness, he saw the revolting smiles of Moore and Bargewood. He wondered how long those terrible images would remain in his mind. How often would they appear in his dreams? It was a situation which *had* to be remedied.

Once the rain had subsided, Peter found a small patch of sand within the pebbles and stones, and began to dig a deep hole with his skeleton hands. As he dug further down, he began to claw at the sand with his nails in order to reach deeper. Then, with tenderness and delicacy, he lowered Darwin's body into his grave and gently filled the hole in with sand. Finally, Peter stood at the grave and gazed down. He wanted to say something. A creature who gave such friendship deserved to be honoured. However, Peter could say nothing, when he wanted to say so much. Instead, he simply stood motionless looking over the grave and allowed the wind to dry his tears.

By the time Peter had freed all of his tears, when no more emotion would come from within his broken little body, it was almost lunch time. He was aware that his Mum and Dad would, no doubt, have received a call from the headteacher informing them of his hasty departure from the assembly hall that morning. He knew that Mum and Dad would be out looking for him, and he knew that he would not be able to explain the situation to them, not until their anger had subsided. Feeling numb inside, he wandered in a kind of hypnotic stupor along the beach. He barely noticed himself tripping over pebbles and stones, he scarcely noticed the sound of the sea or the chirps of low flying oystercatchers and looked ahead without really seeing anything. He had not the faintest idea where he was walking to; he just walked. His feet carried him up the beach and back up through the town where once again he seemed not to give any thought or recognition to the things around him, people, cars, sounds, anything. Finally, he arrived back at the school. He walked through the gates without ceremony and made his way to the playing field where the pupils were on their lunch break. A number of simultaneous football matches were being played by boys with their white shirts hanging out, while girls congregated unwisely behind the goals. Peter wandered through each match, still oblivious to the world around him. Such was his state, a ball kicked at his back by the cowardly Owen Evans, barely registered. Still he walked until, in the middle of a game at the far end of the field, he saw Moore and Bargewood. He walked toward them with a poker face that could earn him millions. Once he caught the gaze of Bargewood he fixed his stare upon him mercilessly. Moore made the mistake of making a sarcastic comment.

'Hey, look,' he shouted, 'It's the bird man of St David's.'

Bargewood, however, was quieter. He watched uneasily as Peter headed up toward him, still with his stone cold eyes fixed on him. Other pupils noticed Peter's trance and soon his movement toward Moore and Bargewood began to attract the morbid attention of those nearby. Finally, Peter arrived at the feet of Bargewood. He stared him squarely in the eye without seeing anything at all. Then, as if some external force had possessed his body, Peter threw a punch which landed with such ferocity on Bargewood's nose that it triggered a loud cracking noise. The nose was broken and the blood began to fall from Bargewood's face before his body hit the ground. Bargewood was out cold. Moore ran to check on his friend.

'Adam!' he cried. 'Are you ok, can you hear me?'

Peter, still in his rage dragged Moore off by his coat and turned the boy onto his back and began to plant blows into Moore's face. Kelly made futile attempts to fight back against the onslaught, but Peter was filled with a rage which could not be contained. The assault was relentless. Edward Jones tried to no avail, to ply Peter off Kelly Moore, who was by this time sobbing and bleeding profusely from his eyes and lips. Peter scarcely showed any emotion at all as he delivered blow after blow. By the time a large congregation of spectators had arrived and circled the action, Peter's knuckles were bleeding. With each and every punch he relived every wrong that had been done to him by Moore and Bargewood – the beatings they had administered, the comments in the corridor, the threats made in the dinner hall, the spits in the face, the tripping in the geography lessons, the wet towels in the changing rooms, the lunch money thefts and so much more. But, as Moore cowered and pleaded with Peter to stop, a vision of Darwin's little body laying dead in the cave appeared in Peter's mind. With the vision lingering in his head, Peter planted one final blow straight to Moore's cheekbone, just as Mr Spencer, the PE teacher, dragged Peter off Moore. Peter did not struggle. He did not resist as Spencer held him firmly by the arm. His work was done.

'Go and ask the secretary to phone for an ambulance, Jenkins!' bellowed Spencer. 'Now!'

Peter watched Barry Jenkins sprint to the office to comply with Mr Spencer's order and looked at Moore and Bargewood lying on the ground. The former cried like a child while the latter still had not moved or made a sound.

'What the hell was that about?' demanded Mr Spencer.

Peter said nothing. He simply stared with vacant eyes at Moore and Bargewood and listened to his heartbeat echoing through his body. Spencer dispersed the young voyeurs back to their football games as he kept hold of Peter's arm and watched as the faint beginnings of a smile appeared on the boy's face.

8
Scan

The waiting room was sterile. The receptionist, a greying woman in her late fifties, was warm and kind with genial smile and gentle manner. She took Anwyn's details and showed her to her chair in the corner of the non-descript room by a window which overlooked an even less inspiring view – the car park. The receptionist offered Anwyn a choice of magazines which was as appealing as the procedure she was about to undertake, however she kept her sarcasm in check and thanked the woman politely. Anwyn scanned through the women's magazines without reading anything at all. Even if she had been inclined to read about ten different kinds of cancer a woman is likely to get in old age, her mind was elsewhere. She couldn't hold a thought down for more than a few seconds or so, and each thought progressed indeterminately with no natural chain. One moment she would be thinking about Michael, then before she had chance to build a picture of him in her mind, nugatory considerations such as the morning's shopping list would emerge, only to be replaced by thoughts of the work that needed to be done on the boat. Her thoughts were like butterflies, flitting and fluttering from here to there and all points in between. Such was her distance from the present that she didn't hear her name being called by a petite nurse with a beautifully lyrical Welsh accent. The nurse repeated.

'Oh, I'm sorry dear,' said Anwyn, 'I was off in my own little world.'

The nurse smiled warmly. 'That's quite alright.'

Anwyn was shown into a changing area where she removed her clothes, dumping them in an untidy heap on the floor. She slipped on a hospital gown and made her way into a space-age room, bright with lights, flashing buttons and brilliant white walls. In the middle of the otherworldly scene was a huge circular structure with a small tunnel in the middle.

'Right, my love,' said the nurse, 'there's nothing to worry about here. All we are going to do is to take a kind of picture of your brain.'

Anwyn joked nervously. 'I hope you have a long lens, my dear.'

'Oh, you're just being modest, I'm sure. All we are going to do is to take a detailed photo of all parts of the brain. All you need to do is to lie down…'

'…And think of England?'

The nurse smiled again, 'I was going to say, relax.'

The nurse aided Anwyn on to a long flat area and eased her down on her back. She placed her hands at her side and angled the head into the correct position. The nurse then squeezed Anwyn's hand reassuringly and left the room to take up her position in an adjoining control booth. Gentle beeps and pips were replaced by honking alarm sounds as the machine slowly pulled Anwyn into its mouth. Despite the soothing words from the nurse, Anwyn began to feel frightened. Her heart began to race and she struggled to regulate her breathing. Like a child she closed her eyes and hoped the fear might pass. Within the darkness she tried to shut out all of the noises around her. The beeps disappeared, as did the pips and soon the honking sounds modulated into the hooting of car horn. It was the comical call of the Morris Minor Traveller. Michael was hooting from inside the car, urging a younger Anwyn to hurry up.

'I'm coming! I'm coming!' she yelled, as she closed the front door and ran through the front garden of their London home, as a warm summer deluge fell upon her.

'Right,' said Michael as Anwyn slumped into the front passenger seat, wiped the rain off her face and closed the door, 'are you ready?'

'Yes, but tell me where we are going!'

'All will be revealed, just show a little patience.'

Anwyn watched as the high-rise buildings of the London metropolis began to disappear in favour of summer rapeseed fields, large expanses of wild poppies and the flat swathes of the Cambridgeshire and Norfolk Fens. Soon, the only structures of any notable height were the giant electricity pylons which conga-ed along the billiard table landscape. The sound of BBC Radio Three, always the preferred choice in the daytime, gifted the two travellers with the delicate tones of Rachmaninov's second piano concerto, the slow movement seeming to slow the world itself down. The ubiquitous pigeons of the city soon gave way to herons standing near meandering rivers, lapwings congregating in fallow fields and kestrels hovering above their prey hiding in summer crops.

Heading past the West Norfolk town of Kings Lynn, they continued to drive along single-file lanes toward the tiny village of West Acre.

'Where are we going?' asked Anwyn for the tenth time.

Michael, enjoying the excitement he was building in the car finally gave in. 'Do you remember our wedding?'

'Of course,' said Anwyn.

'Tell me about it.'

Anwyn looked a little confused, 'Why?'

'Indulge me,' he smiled.

'Well, it was an interesting day to say the least. Not exactly the way we planned it. It was a hot June day and that put the violinist out of tune so the music sounded dreadful. My father made a speech which bore no resemblance to the life we had led up to that point, the registrar fainted in the heat and the hotel threw out our wedding cake before we had chance to eat any of it. There were family feuds. Your aunt Shelly refused to sit next to my uncle Sebastian, she said he was a communist. My second-cousin Frank got drunk and tried to see how many egg mayonnaise sandwiches he could fit into his underpants.'

'Yes,' confirmed Michael. 'So, we are going to try again, this time, just you and me.'

'What d'you mean?'

'You and I are going to renew our vows.' Anwyn's face lit like the sun creeping through the summer clouds. 'If that's okay with you?' Anwyn had no need to answer, she simply reached over and hugged Michael as he drove.

By now the destination was of little importance to Anwyn and her constant questioning as to the location dissipated. It was all about the occasion. Finally, after ambling slowly along a tiny country lane, over a small bridge that crossed a tributary which would eventually lead to the river Nar, they came upon a layby by the entrance to a forest path. By now the clouds had completely cleared, leaving space for a brilliant summer sun to shine, casting shafts of light through the trees and on to the forest floor. The sound of bird song echoed through the trees; blackbirds, sparrows, noisy wrens and even cuckoos called their names. Yet only a solitary treecreeper could be seen, as it darted up and down a tree, searching for invertebrates in the bark with its quirky beak. The ground beneath their feet was littered with pine needles and cones, which softened the ground to the extent that their footsteps barely made a sound as they walked. Eventually, the forest path gave way to a large clearing, a beautiful summer meadow of long grass and wild flowers, buzzing to the sound of industrious bees and waving in the lightest of breezes. At one end of the clearing was a lake belonging to a stately home which could be seen in the distance, while at the other end stood a small stone folly under the shadow of over-hanging trees. The temple-like structure had worn and there were crumbling steps leading up to a raised platform, beneath a roof whose skeletal timber beams could be seen clearly from inside. At either side of the entrance, stone pillars rose to support the weight of the slate roof and wooden trusses. Inside the folly there was an arched-shaped recess which, no doubt had once housed some secular artifact at some point. It was not a house of God. On their arrival at the folly Michael and Anwyn stood and admired the surroundings.

'So, what do we do now?' asked Anwyn

'We wait for the man,' replied Michael.

'What man?'

'That man,' said Michael pointing to a smartly dressed gentleman emerging from the forest path with a briefcase in his hand. He walked toward the lovers, panting and out of breath and sweating profusely in his pin-striped suit.

'Good afternoon, Mr and Mrs Jones, I presume?' Handshakes were exchanged, 'My name is Brock, Samuel Brock.' Pleasantries were shared before Brock finally asked, 'Right shall we start?'

Anwyn and Michael stood on the steps of the folly and smiled at each other. The genial Brock had gentle dulcet tones, although the words themselves passed Anwyn in a blur of contentment. She repeated his words about honour, love and cherishing without really taking them in. All she could do was look at Michael, his imperfections – the slightly crooked nose, the receding hairline, the stubbled complexion and even the way his shirt wasn't tucked in properly – all served to make him perfect. She held his hand and squeezed tightly, lest there was any chance she might lose him. The sun shone beams of light on him as if streaming directly from heaven. Within the exquisiteness of the afternoon, promises were made, vows were renewed and poems were read, before Brock permitted them to kiss. Anwyn closed her eyes and leaned in, but could not feel the warmth of Michael's lips. The sounds of cackling Jays subsided, the cuckoo's call was silenced and the laughter of the woodpecker disappeared, only to be replaced by the beeping sound of the medical equipment surrounding Anwyn.

'It's okay,' said the nurse, 'we're all done, Mrs Jones. Just relax.'

Twenty minutes later, after the friendly receptionist had brought a hot cup of tea, which was swiftly consumed, Anwyn was invited the meet with the neurologist, Dr Chalke. Sporting some designer stubble and a slim-fitting suit, he offered Anwyn the warmest smile and showed her into a non-descript white-painted room. As he settled himself, she observed that the only things adorning the bland walls were a host of framed certificates confirming the genial doctor's credentials.

'I am sorry to have kept you waiting, Mrs Jones,' he said sincerely. 'I'm afraid we're a little short-staffed today. But you are here anyway. Please, take a seat.'

Anwyn sat down nervously. 'Thank you.'

'Now, you have been referred to me by your GP,' he said placing a pair of thin rimmed glasses on his face and perusing Anwyn's file, 'due to concerns regarding memory recollection. Is that right?'

'I don't know,' she said, straight-faced, 'I can't remember why he sent me here. Which doctor?'

Dr Chalke looked a little confused, then, as he saw a mischievous grin start to form at the corners of Anwyn's mouth, he chuckled.

'Well, there's nothing wrong with your humour, Mrs Jones. And believe me, it's good to have a joke in this place.'

'That's what is wrong with the world today,' said Anwyn, 'nobody is funny anymore. Nobody is laughing. Even the so-called comedians are about as much fun as a sandy vibrator.' Chalke was amazed that such words should come forth from the lips of such a seemingly "normal" old lady. 'It's my belief that everybody should do something silly everyday of their life. You know, fart in church, sneeze into the pick and mix sweet counter at the supermarket. I do it. I do it every day. Only this morning I stopped in the town centre and asked a policeman if he could direct me to the erogenous zone. The world is full of grey and beige people with lips that neither go up nor down, frown or smile. They just exist. Those are the best people to play tricks on...'

Anwyn paused for a while, she realised that she was talking aimlessly in order to evade talking about that which was worrying her. Chalke seemed to be enjoying the show, while Anwyn felt acutely embarrassed.

'I'm sorry,' she said, 'I am not great in hospitals.'

'Neither am I,' joked Dr Chalke. 'Look, don't worry yourself until we know everything for sure.' Anwyn nodded, unconvincingly. 'Right, now I just want to ask you a few questions.'

Far from the chirpy, joking woman who had entered the room, the frightened Anwyn appeared and became more and more apparent as Dr Chalke asked a plethora of questions regarding Anwyn's lifestyle, diet, medical history and lineage, as well as stepping delicately into her private life. She told Dr Chalke about Michael and her fears of losing him all over again. Even while filling in his paperwork, Dr Chalke seemed to somehow exude a sense of compassion, which helped put Anwyn at ease.

'Okay,' he said, 'Now, I'd just like to ask you a few questions, to test the memory so to speak.'

'Uh...okay.'

'Now, I'd like you to remember the following address,' Anwyn readied herself. 'Twenty-seven Mulberry Close.'

'Okay.'

'Can you repeat that for me please?' asked Dr Chalke.

Anwyn did so. 'Now I'd like you to remember the phrase, "the early bird catches the worm." Repeat that please.' Anwyn obliged one again. Next, he laid a piece of paper on the desk in front of her and gave another instruction in a clear and precise voice. 'Now, with your left hand I want you to pick up this piece of paper and on it I want you to draw a rectangle and a square.' Anwyn did so. 'Now I would like you to count back from five to one, please.' With a sigh of trepidation, Anwyn did as she was asked. 'Very good, thank you Anwyn. One final question, can you tell me the name of the street which I asked you to repeat at the start of the test?'

'The street?' asked Anwyn, her forehead starting to perspire a little.

'Yes please.'

'It's name?'

'Yes,' replied Chalke.

'You want me to remember it?'

Dr Chalke could see that Anwyn was biding her time, but continued to show understanding. 'Yes, please.'

Anwyn searched her mind but nothing presented itself to her. She looked around the room for clues, knowing full well that there weren't any.

'Was it…' she closed her eyes tightly, trying to find the answer within the darkness of her mind. 'Was it… Was it fifty-seven… Moray Street?'

The awkwardness that followed was tangible, as Dr Chalke looked for a gentle way of informing his patient that she was wrong, while Anwyn, who *knew* she was wrong searched for a way to respond which would save face for both of them. Finally, Dr Chalke broke the silence.

'Very good, Anwyn,' he said. 'Well done.'

Huw, Maggie and Peter sat in silence at the kitchen table. The journey home from the school, via the police station, had been awkward to say the least. The school had suspended Peter for three weeks and had supplied him with all the school work that he had to complete in that time. All Peter wanted was to go to his room, but he knew that he would have to explain his actions first. Where to begin? Huw stared at Peter, waiting for his son to talk, while Maggie sat with her head in her hands.

'Well say something then,' said Huw. 'Go on, talk to me. Tell me what happened. Tell me why you knocked a pupil clean out and broke another boy's nose. Tell me where that all came from. What started it? They're going to press charges. Do you understand what that means? Do you realise the consequences? Do you really know what you have done?' Peter sat perfectly still and in complete silence. 'Answer me!' Huw's angry yell startled Maggie.

'I'm sorry,' whispered Peter from behind waves of quickening trembles.

'I don't care if you are sorry or not!' said Huw rising from the table. He turned Peter's chair around so as to face him and yelled, 'Why did you do it?'

Maggie interjected. 'Huw! Stop shouting!'

'Why?' repeated Huw, completely ignoring his wife.

'Huw, stop it!' screamed Maggie now with a solitary tear running down her face.

'I just want him to speak to me, for Christ's sake!'

Maggie tried to pull her husband away from Peter. 'Well he's not going to speak to you while you are screaming in his face, is he?'

In one last attempt to pull Peter out of his silence, Huw placed his hands on Peter's boney shoulders, shook them violently and cried, 'TALK TO ME!'

'What do you want me to say?' erupted Peter, pushing the kitchen chair over. 'Do you want me to tell you that I did it for fun, that I did it for a laugh with my friends? Well I don't have any friends, Dad! Do want me to say that it's just a phase I'm going through, that I'll soon grow out of it. Or do you want me to tell you about the piss in my lunchbox? Do you want to hear about the time they kept stabbing me in the arm with a compass? Do you want me to tell you about the kickings and the punches? They're always somewhere where the marks can't be seen, the ribs perhaps or a dead leg, that's a good one. Do you want to hear about them dragging me into the showers and soaking me in all my clothes? "But don't tell anyone Peter", they would say. And who could I tell anyway? The teachers? They don't care.'

Huw and Maggie were startled into paralysed stillness as they listened to their son's harrowing revalations.

'What about us?' said Maggie, with a voice softening and shaking beneath her weep.

'You?' he laughed sarcastically. 'You have enough to deal with without me. And why would I talk? This is not a house for talking. It's a house of whispers, when you both argue in the bedroom at night so that I can't hear. Well, I hear it. All of it! When you thought I was sleeping, I was listening. I never sleep. I just think about what the next day at school will bring. I wonder what they will do to me next. Well, what they did today was to kill the one bloody thing that made my life worth living. They killed Darwin.'

Peter ran out of the kitchen, ignoring the calls from his

parents to return, and slammed the front door behind him.

Huw concluded that Peter would be back as soon as his stomach needed a refill. Maggie on the other hand was ready to call the police, believing that, in his current state he could do anything. However, Huw was adamant that neither should go chasing him, 'He just wants the attention,' he said. Peter ran until his legs were leaden with weariness, out of the town, along the costal path, down to the beach and along to Darwin's grave. He sat down as the sun began to set in the stillness of the evening. He sat popping the air sacks in the seaweed strewn over the rocks following the previous night's high tide, and thought about everything that was happening in his life. He thought about the bullying, the marital disharmony in his home, his loneliness and, of course Darwin. Suddenly, he was startled out of his thoughts.

'What are you doing, Peter?' said a familiar voice.

'Anwyn, you frightened me!' replied Peter. 'Where's Byron?'

Byron came bounding over the rocks and seaweed and leapt onto Peter licking his face with delight.

'Someone's pleased to see you!' said Anwyn. 'So, what *are* you doing here?'

'I ran away,' he replied. 'I'm in trouble at home. We had an argument. I don't know if I'm going back.'

'I see.' Anwyn perched herself down on a rock. She noticed the dedication on the cave wall. 'And who was Darwin?'

'He was my friend.'

'He was a small fellow then?' she joked, referring to the tiny grave.

'He was a bird, a puffin,' he said defiantly, 'but he was *still* my friend.'

Anwyn was apologetic. 'I didn't mean to make light of it. Forgive me.'

Peter gazed down at the grave again. 'He never told me what I could or couldn't do. He never let me down. He just let me... talk and he listened. I could talk to him about anything. He didn't judge me. He never called me *weirdo*.'

Byron seemed to know, as most dogs instinctively do, that Peter needed affection. This time he curtailed his exuberance and gently licked the boy's hand, before snuggling into his chest.

'I had an imaginary friend,' said Anwyn, stroking Byron's back as he rested. 'Her name was Emily. I always wanted to be called Emily, I hate the name Anwyn. I never forgave my Mum for that. Anyway, Emily was so real to me. I could hear her voice in my head. She had a funny little giggle, very high-pitched. She used to get me into trouble at the dinner table. She would make me laugh. She once told me to put salt in the sugar tin. Ha! We fell out over that one, I had to do chores for a week.'

'Why are you telling me all this?' asked Peter

'I don't know.' Anwyn dragged her windswept hair behind her ears. 'I suppose I'm telling you so... so you know that *I* know what it's like to be alone.'

'That's not going to bring Darwin back though, is it?'

Anwyn thought for a moment. 'No, but then nothing will. If that's what you're waiting for... well, you'll be waiting for a long time.'

Peter wiped a tear away with the cuff of his coat. 'Well, thanks for cheering me up!'

'Look, what I mean is, you need a real friend.'

'I had a real friend, he's dead.'

'No, you had a bird which you loved, very much… and you wanted it to love you too.'

Peter snapped, 'He did love me.'

'How do you know, Peter?'

'I just do, okay!'

'Let me just ask you this.' Anwyn spoke as gently as possible. 'How did he tell you he loved you? That shopping trolley, is that what you put him in?' Peter rolled his eyes and turned his head away, a confession of sorts. 'And why did you do that? Did you do it so that he wouldn't escape or so you knew where he was, when you needed him?' Peter shrugged his shoulders. 'You see, your Darwin, like my Emily wasn't really a friend. They were just a kind of one way relationship that we both created so that we wouldn't get hurt… again?'

'I don't understand.'

'Yes, you do,' Anwyn replied compassionately. 'I know you feel alone at home and I know your parents know that too. So you latched on… no, that's not it, forgive me… you sought love and friendship in such a way that *you* could control the relationship. A real friend would challenge you. A true friend would make you question yourself. You see a friendship is a two way thing.'

Anwyn dragged herself up gingerly and called to Byron. She did her coat up and once gain battled the breeze by pushing her hair back behind her ears.

'I suppose that's why I'm telling you all of this. I'm challenging you now. Not because I want to make things harder for you, but because … because I'm your friend.'

Peter turned his head back to Anwyn and offered an acknowledging smile from one corner of his mouth.

'Thanks,' he said.

'You know where I am,' said Anwyn walking off. A few steps later she turned back to Peter and said, 'Just don't bring that bloody spider!'

9
Offending Christians

Two weeks passed by. During that period everyone seemed to fall into a stupor of stillness. Huw and Maggie, try as they might, still could not connect to each other on anything other than a cordial level. Peter kept himself to himself, although did on one occasion visit Anwyn to deliver some shopping from the town. This led to a game of chess and cup of tea, and Anwyn once again reiterated her friendship. As for Anwyn, she waited for her test results and continued to exhibit problems with her memory. Night after night she listened to the poetry on the wireless and each night it seemed to give a little more solace. However, every iota of that solace was stolen with each lapse in her memory.

On a tempestuous Monday morning, Maggie guided Anwyn carefully by the arm, along a gravel path which led to the entrance of St David's Cathedral. Anwyn, as ever, protested. 'I can walk you know!' she moaned. They made it inside just in time. As soon as they stepped inside the main entrance the heavens opened and a wild deluge fell on the tiny city.

'What are we doing here?' asked Anwyn.

'I thought you might like to stop and have a wander around...' Anwyn looked around and offered little more than a snarl of indifference, despite the grandeur of her surroundings. '...and get a cup of tea...' Anwyn was still unimpressed. '...and a cake.' Having pacified Anwyn's sweet tooth, Maggie picked up an information leaflet and began to stroll through the cathedral with the old girl in tow.

'I've been here so many times before, but I still forget which part is which unless I have the leaflet,' said Maggie making small talk.

'Right, so which bit are we in now?' said Anwyn trying to show a little interest.

'Maggie looked at the map on the back of the leaflet, 'This is the nave.'

'Oh, I see.'

'It's where the congregation sit. But surely you remember being here as a child.'

'I can't even remember if I put my underwear on this morning, and you want me to remember that far back.'

Maggie was apologetic. 'I didn't mean to make light of...'

'Oh, go on with you!' said Anwyn.

'When do you get the results back from the hospital?'

'I have to see the doctor tomorrow.'

'Are you scared?'

Anwyn paused for a moment. 'Shall we grab a pew?' Maggie smiled and sat down on the hard wooden benches, uneasily. 'Yes, I'm scared.'

'What are you most afraid of?'

'Oh, where to start?' said Anwyn. 'I always thought that as one grew older fear would dissipate somewhat. I thought you'd get more confident because you'd know more. But it doesn't work like that at all. You do learn, but each thing you learn seems to be accompanied by more questions. So you end up knowing more, but feeling more uncertain.'

'And that's what's frightening you now,' asked Maggie, 'the uncertainty?'

'Yes.' Anwyn gave a weary sigh. 'What will I remember? What will I forget? But most of all what will I remember of Michael. Each night I try to force myself to remember something about him. I try to recall a different memory as I'm falling asleep. I'm very good at the long-term stuff, but what will happen when that goes too? I keep looking at pictures and holding tiny slides up to the light, trying to save his image in my head. It's strange, if it is Alzheimer's, I am not at all frightened about me. I don't care if I piss myself, I don't care if I forget to put my shoes on to do the shopping, but if I lose Michael … again… that would be intolerable.'

Maggie placed her hand on Anwyn's. 'I wish I knew what to say.'

'There's nothing you can say. You can just be here with me, that's more than enough for me.'

'I'll say a prayer for you if you like.'

Anwyn took exception to Maggie's flippant remark. 'No, thank you! I don't go in for all that mumbo jumbo. It's a load of old crap. Religion is for the weak.'

'What ever do you mean?' asked Maggie incredulously. 'And keep your voice down, you might offend someone.'

'Good!' said Anwyn in an even louder voice.

'Anwyn please!'

'They are *exactly* the sort of people who deserve to be offended; people who have to be told what to do, "well if it's God's will…" what a load of old crap. Don't they have a will of their own?'

'I don't think it's as simple as that. I think it's more…'

Anwyn hadn't quite finished. '…And all that pompous crap about God loving us! "God loves everyone!" Oh yes, he really loves those little children with bone cancer, he really loves all those disabled people.'

'Anwyn, please!'

'Where was he when the Jews were murdered? Where was he during the bloody Black Death?'

Maggie took hold of Anwyn's arm, 'Anwyn, stop it!'

'Where is he now?' she shouted.

A trio of Japanese tourists and a couple of local ramblers, admiring the tall stained-glass windows, turned around and stared for a second before mumbling to each other.

'What are you looking at?' she said to the couple, before addressing the Japanese onlookers. 'And you can bugger off too!'

Anwyn stood up and wandered off down the aisle, leaving Maggie at a loss as to what to do. She apologised to the ramblers and the tourists for Anwyn's outburst and followed on. Maggie kept a safe distance away from Anwyn for fear of triggering another outburst.

Finally, Anwyn made her way to the cathedral refectory. She ordered two teas from a quaint, mild-mannered young girl with straight brown hair and a kindly face. Having fumbled her loose change from out of her tatty leather purse, a relic from a trip to Paris with Michael in the sixties, Anwyn took her place at a table for two and waited for the girl to arrive with the order. While she waited Anwyn considered her outburst. She felt humiliation for making a spectacle of herself, she regretted putting Maggie in such an uncomfortable position, but she looked in her heart and could find no remorse for the things she had said. She looked around at the majestic fusion of Romanesque and English Gothic architecture, the intricate carvings and the ornate windows, and tried to reconcile the fact that everything around her had been assembled in the name of a God that nobody had any proof of. A God whom she believed was uncaring, unkind and unjust. If only, she thought, people could put such faith and love in each other.

The tea finally arrived just as Maggie approached the table and took her coat off.

'You okay?' she asked.

'Yes, I got you tea, is that alright?'

'Fine.' Maggie hung her coat on the back of her chair and sat down.

'I'm sorry.'

'What was that all about?'

'I don't know,' said Anwyn, 'I'm just angry. Maybe I just needed someone to blame.'

'For what?' asked Maggie.

'For losing Michael, for losing my mind… I don't know. I don't know why I got so angry. You see God is as real to me as the Loch Ness Monster or Big Foot. But someone… or something has to be responsible for taking Michael away.'

'But, why?'

'What do you mean?' asked Anwyn.

'I mean, why does someone need to be blamed?'

Anwyn ruminated deeply, searching her intellect for a

respectable answer. 'Everything happens for a reason.'

'Maybe.' Maggie poured some tea into the two mugs, spilling a little on the table. 'Maybe not. But blaming someone, or something... it's not going to bring them back...' Anwyn took a sip of her tea, 'is it?'

'It just doesn't make sense, Maggie; any of it. If I could make sense of it then...'

Maggie afforded Anwyn the courtesy of a little thinking time. 'Then, what?'

'Then maybe I wouldn't hurt so much.'

Maggie reached across the table and held Anwyn's hand, before placing a soft kiss on her cold, aging knuckles. She looked in to Anwyn's eyes with a love that the old girl had not felt for years. Anwyn smiled and looked around and saw that the Japanese tourists, who by now had made their way to a table on the other side of the refectory, were staring at them. Anwyn considered a curt response, but with her rage ameliorated, simply turned back to Maggie and whispered to her.

'Go easy on the public kisses, my dear,' she said. 'We wouldn't want the Tenko trio to think you were engaged in some kind of extra-generational lesbian affair, would we?'

Maggie giggled beneath her breath and much to Anwyn's delight, waved at the Japanese tourists who, in turn, waved back awkwardly.

'Let's take a drive into town, I fancy a little retail therapy,' said Maggie.

'Where?'

'Let's go into Swansea, we can wander around the market if you like?'

'I'd like that,' replied Anwyn, 'but I can't leave Byron alone for too long.'

'That's okay, I'll ask Huw to stop by. Do you have a spare key?'

'Yes, there's one underneath a flower pot, if you're sure it's not too much trouble.'

Maggie pulled out her mobile phone and sent a text to her husband. 'Done!' she announced, 'Let's splurge!'

Peter sat beside his father as the Dolphin Watch motorboat, complete with two Americans, and a sexagenarian couple from Norfolk, rushed across the water in search of Common, Risso and Bottlenose Dolphins, Atlantic Grey Seals or even, if they were particularly lucky, a Basking Shark. He listened to his father talking to the passengers about the wildlife and the fragility of the ecosystem off the west coast of Wales. He spoke with such authority and passion. He hadn't seen that side of his father for a long time. The only image he had of his father in his head was that of the extra-marital kiss with Emma, who also took her place in the boat. It lingered in his head every time he saw his father come home from work. Peter wondered if he would ever really see his father again. He couldn't un-see what he had seen, but he hoped that he might be able to learn to live with it, and maybe even forgive him. However, his suspension from school following the attack on Darwin's killers had only served to widen the chasm between the two and as they bounced along the waves to the sound of the Norfolk gentleman vomiting over the side of the boat, he felt further away from his father than ever before. As the horizon tipped left and then right Peter's eyes strayed into the distance where he saw the lighthouse, beautiful in its isolation, reaching out from the sea and climbing up into the sky of dull white.

What a perfect place to live, he thought. There would be no Moores or Bargewoods, no cutting comments, no need to worry about anything other than turning the giant light on and off, and to guide the ships safely into to bay. The rest of the time he could spend watching the wildlife; the gannets, the porpoises, the skuas, the dolphins and, of course, the puffins. However, he also thought about Anwyn's words. In such a lonely and isolated life there would be nobody to challenge him, to question his thoughts or to simply bring a different perspective on life. If only things could be simple as nature. As cruel and as crooked as nature could be, its cruelty came from necessity rather than inclination. The skuas take the puffin chicks from their burrowed nests not for fun, but to feed their own. He had read enough, tender in years though he was, by Charles Darwin to understand that animals of the same breed often attacked and killed each other in the pursuit of a safe place to live or for the affections of a mate, but in both cases violence and cruelty was essential to ensure the survival of the species. Cruelty by inclination, he ascribed, was singular to the human condition. People were unnecessarily complicated. They love, but with a host of conditions, they kill not simply to survive or to protect, but in avarice, for revenge and because of their ignorance and stupidity. He hated the complexity of his feelings toward his father. On the one hand he loved him with all the love he had, while on the other he hated him for the pain he had put his mother through. He was proud of his father but felt his humiliation having caught him in his adultery. As the spray from the sea rose up from the waves and salted his face, he wondered if life could ever be as simple as nature.

119

10
The Lighthouse

Moments are connected. They are linked together by coincidence or if you believe in such things, fate, destiny or God. However, such happenings go completely un-noticed yet they may, if even for the briefest of moments, connect us.

The mid-morning café was empty but for a solitary waitress and a somewhat contemplative Maggie. In the background, from behind the counter, banal pop music was followed by equally annoying radio commercials, selling everything from half-price primulas at the Red Dragon Garden Centre to a months free membership when you join the St David's snooker club. The content was soon lost on Maggie as she sipped her latte after a day at work. The thought of going home was not one that she relished. The awkwardness between Huw and her was beginning to solidify into an immovable and impregnable emotional block, one which would not permit love to enter or to leave. The close relationship she had had for many years with her son was at risk due to Peter's propensity to secrecy, isolation and angry outbursts. Only her unlikely friendship with Anwyn seemed to provide any solace, although she knew that the old girl was unpredictable to say the least. Looking into the stirred swirls of her beverage she sighed and looked around and within for an answer.

Hanging at a slightly crooked angle on an adjacent wall was a watercolour painting of Small's Lighthouse beneath a calming midday sun. The diluted vibrancy of colour in the unimaginatively titled *Afternoon at Small's Lighthouse,* seemed to mirror the anaemic hues in her own face, as she contemplated that which she swore she would never do; leave Huw. The lighthouse, with its soft tones and gentle brush strokes, seemed to reach out to her, pulling her into the serenity of its world. It seemed to call out to her into a domain which would be exclusively hers. The years of maternal and marital service had come at a cost. She wondered who was she? Who was the woman behind the kindness? Who was the woman behind the commitments? How much more than a wife and a mother had she become? She wondered if, after all the years of caring for others, what she had left for herself. The lighthouse stood alone, tall and strong, in the middle of the tempestuous waves of the Irish Sea; could *she* stand alone? She stirred her tea and, for a moment, indulged the idea that, maybe, she needed a new start.

For some inexplicable reason Anwyn switched on the mid-morning radio. The gentle-voiced female radio announcer allowed the eleven o'clock pips to sound then introduced the next programme.

'Now, in a change to our scheduled programme we join Katherine Mallory for a repeat of Verse Nightly.'

The dulcet tones of the unlikely but familiar voice of Mallory came through the warm speakers of the radiogram. A strange choice for the middle of the morning, she thought, yet Anwyn embraced the moment. She put the kettle on and made a cup of tea. As she listened to the familiar poems of Keats and Shelley without particular satisfaction, Byron sat at her feet, licking his paws. However, as she moved over to the window to gaze out over the sea beneath, her attention was grabbed by a familiar name.

'Following an overwhelming response to his previous works,' said the lulling Mallory, 'we now come to another poem by Jack Newton.' Anwyn turned and looked at the radiogram for a moment. 'This poem, read by Henton Phillips, is called, *The Lighthouse.*'

Anwyn's gaze returned to the ocean, to the little lighthouse rising up from the waters into a greying sky, as she listened to the deep, yet smooth timbre of Henton Phillips' voice and allowed the words to seep through her.

The Lighthouse

Rising from the salt and surf,
Through the Westerlies ire,
Standing stoic but so quiet,
And never to tire.

Turning shafts of guiding light
Will see you home again,
Through all the gods may throw at you
To soothe your every pain.

And somewhere deep inside you,
The lighthouse rises strong,
Illuminating you with love
Through days dark and long.

How it came to be there
Or how it came to shine
Should not concern you friend,
Just know that all is fine.

At that moment, Anwyn felt like she could almost reach out and touch Small's Lighthouse. The poem was beautiful to her, though she knew that Michael would never have approved of such simplicity in approach. Michael's taste was more cerebral and, on many a happy occasion, Anwyn had teased her lover. She would call him a snob, he would call her a philistine. He used to claim that the joy in poetry is in fathoming out the content, but Anwyn would argue that that was akin to trying to solve a crossword puzzle. However, the theme of the poem was a comforting one. Perhaps there was something strong within her that could and would guide her through the worries about her short-term memory. But what was it? Was the strength within of her own making or was it a power from something or someone else? The poem hinted at something secular which suited her down to the ground. The thought that she would owe anything to God repulsed her. She wanted nothing to do with him. Was it the soul that Newton alluded to? She had more belief in the concept of the soul as science had not as yet, conclusively disproved it, at least in a way that it had with much of the bible.

She turned the radio off and looked again to the little

lighthouse and felt something warm yet mysterious within her. Ironically, it was an almost religious experience. She looked at it and felt calm, the way, perhaps, a Buddhist might feel when meditating on an image of the enlightened Shakyamuni. Whatever the feeling was, she felt good.

As the clouds covered the sea and the surf began to rise, two people, perhaps souls, began to connect to each other, beyond words, through the lighthouse. As he bobbed up and down on the waves, alone in his boat, Huw stared up at the huge, towering Small's Lighthouse. He looked up and gazed in awe at its defiant strength and marveled that man could build something to withstand the worst that nature could throw at it.

Back on land, in the dull light of his little bedroom, Peter stood before a painting of the very same lighthouse on his wall. As he fixed his gaze on the picture he felt the breeze blow through his hair, he heard the sound of gulls squawking, he could feel tiny droplets of seawater pepper his cheeks and could smell the ocean rising through his nose.

Huw cut the engine on his vessel and allowed the ocean to softly sway him one way, then the other, as though being lulled in the arms of nature. The memory of a deep-voiced man began to surface in his consciousness and he slipped into his thoughts. He saw the vastness of the ocean and heard the excited voice of an infant.

Peter, lost in the picture in his room, heard the voice too. It was *his* voice. He heard it echoing in his memory.

'Daddy, look!' he said, pointing his little hand up to the skies around the lighthouse. 'I can see lots and lots of them. What are they called?'

'Gannets, Peter,' Huw replied in a younger voice, unsullied by the reality of his later paternal tribulations. 'The white ones are called gannets.'

In that moment in time Peter and his father were connected. The memory, which they both experience at exactly the same time, brought them closer together than they had been in a long time. If only they knew it.

The five-year-old Peter ran around the perimeter of the Lighthouse on a little path that stretched round the huge glass panels which surrounded the enormous light at the top of the building. Standing so high above the ground, he felt as though he could see the entire world. He felt he could see all of the sea, all of the land and all of the sky.

Huw picked up the young Peter and placed him on his shoulders.

'Now you're taller than me.'

The little boy laughed, 'Now I can see even more than the whole world, Daddy.'

'I know.'

'Is there any more than the whole world?' asked Peter.

'Yes, I'm sure there is.'

'Is it bigger than the whole world?'

'It's as big as you want it to be, boy.'

There was a little pause, in which the yaps of the terns filled the quiet of the conversation. '… that must be as big as a elephant!'

The sound of Huw's laughter reverberated through two connected minds and memories. At that moment they both felt the warmth of each other's love. Were they not separated by sea and circumstance they would have both run into each other's arms and confirmed their love each other. As it was, they had to be content to relive a moment, however brief, when they were truly happy together, standing at the top of the lighthouse, looking out over the wonder of the world.

Then, the two trains of thought split, down two separate tracks. Peter imagined a cardboard shoebox. As he stood holding it on the circular balcony of the lighthouse, he could hear and feel fidgeting and rustling coming from within. He rested the box on the handrail and slowly lifted the lid. Timidly, Darwin emerged from the darkness of the box and illuminated the world with his striking colours once more. Peter's heart rose, as he finally watched Darwin fly away into the sky, free once more. It was a reverie, but a sweet one.

Huw saw Maggie waiting for him on the rocks at the foot of the lighthouse. Her hair flowed effortlessly, catching each gentle breeze that swept in off the waves. She smiled at him, the way she used to smile, with a hint of mischief and a glint in her eye. She looked the way she did before they made love. Again the dream was sweet, even if it was just a dream.

11
Searching for Jack

It was another interesting day of weather in St David's. The stillness, the wind, the rain challenged the sun while the black, white and grey clouds all fought for supremacy of the skies. Meteorologically speaking, the westernmost part of Wales was never a dull place. Anwyn had been thinking about the poems of Jack Newton. She had been moved by them, but had no way of recalling them other than in her own unreliable memory. There were no bookshops in St David's so she knew she would have to go to Swansea, or better still, Cardiff to find a copy of Newton's work. Using the "interweb" was impossible, as her austere little house wasn't even furnished with a television less so a computer. So she resolved to drive to Cardiff to seek out the work of Jack Newton.

The drive to Cardiff, along the M4 motorway was, as ever, painfully slow; partly due to traffic, partly due to Anwyn's refusal to take the Morris Minor past the fifty miles-per-hour mark. She hugged the inside lane for the entire journey, forcing coaches, trucks and tankers to pass her with angry stares from the drivers. She saw them from the corner of her eye but stoutly refused to acknowledge them. Instead she stared straight ahead with both hands gripping the steering wheel tightly and ignoring to hoots of discontent from around her, while Byron stood with his front paws on the door handle, watching the world go by.

Cardiff was another world. It was a *real* city, a bustling metropolis far removed from the industrial town she had known from previous visits as a child, when the industries were heavy and the streets dark and dull. She remembered the smell of the hops from the famous Brains brewery. She hated it then but as her indeterminate memory triggered a whiff of the fermenting beer, she felt a strange sense of longing for the scent once more. The new Cardiff was very different. High office buildings with tinted glass, elegant shop fronts, immaculately paved streets and all the signs of the modernity that she and Michael had spent their life trying to avoid, were ubiquitously on display.

Having parked up nearby, she walked with Byron down St Mary's Street and came upon a large bookshop. It was a huge literary superstore filled from wall to wall with thousands of volumes of fiction, non-fiction, biographies, autobiographies, audio-books, travel books, children's books, young adult books, erotic books, reference books, military books, sport books, books on entertainment – film, stage, music and art – as well as books on technology, politics, science, religion and much, much more. However, the poetry section was almost non-existent. There were a few copies of Byron, some Donne and even Pam Ayres, along with a couple of general poetry collections but certainly no sign of Jack Newton. This made Anwyn angry. The art of poetry had made her husband the man he was, it sustained their marriage and it gave Anwyn an insight into a great many things; things that mattered – love, truth, happiness, science and beauty. Now the shelves seemed rammed with get-rich quick books, violent novels about violent people and dirty paperbacks which, as Anwyn surmised from reading the preamble on the back of some, seemed to cheapen the very concept of love. Who were the poets of today? Where were they? Did anyone actually write poems anymore?

'Can I help?' said a thin spectacled young girl. Anwyn hated that phrase, because she felt it stemmed not from a desire to help, but rather to earn. When she heard that phrase she actually heard, *can I take your money?*

'Yes, you can dear,' she replied sharply, 'is this really the sum total of your poetry?'

'Um... yes I'm afraid it is,' the girl replied sheepishly, not daring to remind Anwyn that dogs were not permitted in the shop. 'But if there is something you like I could order it in for you.'

'What, and then drive all the way into town again? No thank you.'

'No, we could post it to you if you like.'

Anwyn was pacified a little, 'Oh, well that would be a help.'

The genial assistant showed Anwyn to the customer service counter, then ambled behind the desk and started her computer.

'Okay,' she tapped the keys gently, 'what is the book called?'

'Oh, I don't know,' replied Anwyn.

'Well who is it by?'

'Ah, his name is Jack Newton.'

'And it's a poetry book?'

'Yes.'

The assistant scanned the screen for a while before stating, 'I'm sorry madam but I'm afraid I can't find anybody of that name on our database.'

'Well, he must be there,' said an incredulous Anwyn, 'I heard his poems on the radio.'

'I'm really sorry, but I can't find anyone by that name on the computer.'

'Bugger the computer, you must have heard of him!' she snapped. 'You work in a book shop, don't you? So you should know all about books.'

'Well, I um…'

'Surely you studied about literature and poetry to work here.'

'W-Well n-n-not really…' she stammered, 'I um… I studied nursery teaching.'

'Well, what the bloody hell are you doing here, you silly girl?' The girl looked around to see that dozens of eyes were drawn to the commotion. 'I suppose there is a classical literature student somewhere reading extracts of Homer's Odyssey to a group of bloody three-year olds!'

'Please, Madam you are causing a scene.'

'I don't care!' she shouted. 'I want to see the manager.'

Anwyn received less help from the manager than she did from the shop assistant. Later, she felt slightly guilty for speaking so abruptly to the likable girl, as the manager seemed to know even less about books than his employee. She realized that her anger was merely fuelled by the disappointment of not finding any work by Jack Newton.

Anwyn's aching feet carried her through the streets of

Cardiff throughout the rest of the day, in and out of every book shop she could find, in every nook and cranny of the city. She visited huge franchised stores and little independent shops and even wandered around the indoor market, searching through faded and frayed second-hand books. The response and result were the same each time, only with varying degrees of politeness. Nobody had any idea who Jack Newton was.

Despite a pleasant lunch for one at a quaint little café near St David's Hall, which came complete with the best that Welsh cuisine could offer – a Welsh cake, it had been a wholly unsuccessful day. The drive home seemed to take even longer than the outbound journey. Anwyn's eyes felt heavy and each turn of the un-powered steering wheel seemed to become more and more arduous. However, she felt happy to see the Pembrokeshire coastline come into view once more. It was like seeing an old friend.

She pulled up outside her cottage and rested her head on the steering wheel. Byron, still curled up in the foot-well of the passenger's side, barely stirred. Eventually, he followed Anwyn as she made her way to the front door. As she went to place the key in the lock, she found that the door swung open. She assumed that she had forgotten to lock the house again, however as she went through the house something didn't seem right. There were no signs of a break in, the lock was intact and the windows were unbroken. She stepped slowly through the house and checked that everything was where it should be. She looked in the drawers, the kitchen cupboards and everything seemed fine, yet, still, she felt uneasy. She made her way into her bedroom and everything was as before except for one omission. At the side of her bed, the box containing the slides and 35mm films was missing. A cold sweat came over her and pins and needles of horror consumed her body. Who would want to take them? Why? For the next hour Anwyn tore up her house looking for her slides and films but found nothing. She looked again in the kitchen cupboard, the kitchen units, the fridge and even the tool box. She was acutely aware that, with her mind evidently slipping away, she was liable to put them anywhere. With each disappointment her heart sank lower and lower. Finally, after searching high and low without success, she sat on the edge of her bed and, in the absence of tears, simply stared into the nothing.

It had been a quiet day at the cottage hospital. Other than a visit from Mrs Ainsely who had sprained her ankle and a teacher from the school who had had, in her words, "a funny turn," there had been little to do. Maggie had even had time to nip out for a bite to eat. She sat in the office having another cup of tea when the receptionist interrupted politely.

'Maggie,' she said, 'there is someone with a knife wound in the waiting room.'

'Okay, I'm coming.'

Maggie did a double-take when she realized who was in the waiting area. Sitting with her head bowed, alone in the waiting room was the slim figure of Emma. Had there been anyone else to treat her, Maggie would have requested that Emma be seen by another nurse. However, today that option was not open to her. Emma sat holding her left hand which was wrapped in a blood-stained tea-towel.

'Emma Howitt,' she called. Emma looked up and saw Maggie and her eyes widened in horror. Maggie spoke without feeling but with a coldness that was alien to her. 'Would you follow me please?'

Maggie showed her into a cubicle and without making eye contact, asked her a series of standard questions and marked the answers down on her forms.

'How did you do this?'

'I slipped while holding the carving knife at home. What does it matter? Just stitch me up and I'll get out of your hair.'

'I need to know for the paperwork,' replied Maggie in an unfamiliar and, in truth, unconvincing monotonal voice.

'Are you up to date with your tetanus vaccination?'

'Yes,' answered Emma.

'Are you on any medication at the moment?'

'Yes.'

'What are you taking?' asked Maggie.

'Fluoxetine.' Maggie finally looked up at Emma. The knowledge that Emma was taking anti-depressants split her into two contrasting opinions. Firstly, she felt glad that she was perhaps struggling with the consequences of her kiss with Huw, on the other hand she felt pity for her as well. 'One-hundred and fifty micrograms a day.'

'Do you have any allergies?' asked Maggie. 'Are you okay with plasters and penicillin?'

'No, that's all fine.'

Maggie repressed her natural bedside manner and took Emma's hand. 'Right, show me.'

The wound was long, deep, clean and stretched from one side of the palm of her hand to the other.

'It's going to need stitching.'

'Fine.'

'I'll give you a local anesthetic. It will numb the area in

ten minutes or so. Then I'll sew you up.'

Maggie stepped out of the cubicle and fetched the required medical supplies and came back. She took Emma's hand roughly in her own and began to clean the wound. Emma winced.

'Hold still, please,' said Maggie dispassionately.

Emma, uncomfortable with needles, looked away as Maggie plunged the needle straight into the wound. Once again, Emma winced, but, unwilling to give Maggie the satisfaction of seeing her in pain, she managed not to make a sound despite the discomfort.

'I'll be back in a few minutes when it's had a chance to take effect,' said Maggie as she pulled back the cubicle curtains and stormed out.

While allowing the drugs to numb the sensation in Emma's hand, Maggie went back to her tea and had another sip. As she lifted the cup she noticed that her hand was shaking and she felt uncontrollably tense inside. She tried to settle herself with some deep breaths but it was no use. The anger, the humiliation and the pain in her heart, was such that she could not physically control her emotions. Finally, she returned.

'Right, let me see the hand again.' Emma laid out her hand. 'Keep as still as you can.'

The silence that ensued was uncomfortable for both of them. Both were brimming with words but neither wanted to be the first to speak. Finally, Emma made the first move.

'I *am* sorry you know.'

'Don't!' said Maggie. 'Just don't!'

'I mean it!'

'I don't want to hear it.'

'Please,' Emma implored, 'I just have to…'

'…You don't have to do anything,' interrupted Maggie, pulling roughly on the first stitch, 'you've done quite enough, thank you.'

'I can explain.'

'Of course you can,' said Maggie with more than a hint of sarcasm, 'people like you always do.'

'What do you mean, people like me?' said Emma, firmly.

'People like you, home-breakers, call them what you like, always have an explanation. They tell themselves that there is a reason for doing the things they do, so they don't have to admit to themselves that what they did was…'

Emma pressed Maggie, 'What?'

Maggie couldn't think of an appropriate word. Her mind, in her burning internal ire, was blank. She tugged hard again on a stitch but received little more than a slight grimace from Emma.

'You tried to take my husband, for Christ's sake,' she finally caught Emma's eye. 'What do you want me to say?'

'Nothing,' replied Emma, 'I just want you to listen. I didn't try to take your husband. That's not how it works.'

'Oh, really?'

'I know you hate me,' said Emma, 'and I know you don't hate anyone. I know you are a good person, a good wife…'

'Oh, please!'

'But I'm a good person too, I might have been…' she thought for a moment, '…weak, but that doesn't make me bad. It makes me human.'

'Yeah, right!'

'Yes, at least as human as your husband.' A moment of truth forced Maggie to look at Emma once again. She had no response. 'And you don't think he's a bad person, do you?' Maggie said nothing. 'Otherwise, you would have left him.' Maggie retained her silence. 'Wouldn't you?'

'It's not as simple as that,' replied Maggie, 'especially when there are kids involved.' Emma looked shamefacedly down at the floor. 'Yes, you know exactly what I mean.'

'I had no idea that Peter was going to see what happened,' said Emma.

'Oh, so that makes it all okay then does it?'

'No, it's not okay,' said Emma softly. 'It's far from okay. But it has happened. I can't take it back and neither can Huw. When I kissed him… I knew it wasn't right everything about it was wrong. His lips were firm, I bet when he kisses you they are soft and tender. As he put his arms around me, his hands barely touched me, I imagine that when he touches you, he touches you deeply. I wanted kindness and Huw gives that, freely and unconditionally. I wanted love but I could tell that he could never give it to me. In a strange way I think he kissed me to tell me that there was no chance that anything could become of us.'

'I can't believe I'm hearing this.'

'I just wanted some love, someone to treat me with a little respect.'

'Respect?' said Maggie incredulously, raising her voice. 'You don't deserve respect! You *earn* respect! You don't earn respect by trying to steal someone's husband.'

'I told you,' shouted Emma, 'I didn't try to…'

'…I don't give a shit!' screamed Maggie.

A long silence ensued. They stared at each other for a moment, each refusing to avert their look first. Then, finally in the stillness, Emma swallowed hard and spoke softly.

'I was raped.' Emma looked away. 'There, I said it.'

Maggie was taken aback by the statement. She said

nothing, and allowed Emma the time to expatiate.

'It started after Mum died.' Her voice became measured, almost calm, as if her story had caught a gentle breeze and could float effortlessly toward Maggie. 'I was twelve. It was just my Dad and me. We never talked, not really. After the funeral he just... stopped. He stopped talking, he stopped laughing and he hardly ever smiled anymore. He just used to sit on Mum's side of the bed and stare. I used to get my own tea, my own breakfast, make my school lunch...feed the dog. Mum was a very tactile person. She was always giving cuddles and when she died, all that kind of contact... well, it just stopped. But I still needed it, Dad still needed it, but neither of us could figure it out. Then one night, about midnight, he picked me up out of bed and said he needed a hug. I was half asleep, I just went along with it. He told me he loved me. He held me tight.' Emma's voice began to quiver slightly. 'At first I was happy. I had wanted to be held for so long. Then... then he started to call out my mother's name, over and over again. And he started to touch me. Before I knew it...' Maggie barely blinked as Emma spared her the details. 'It was over.'

'I'm sorry,' said Maggie.

'So am I.' Emma picked out the beginnings of a tear from the corner of her eye. 'He just needed *his* kind of love and I couldn't give it to him, not at that age. But that didn't stop him from trying. I wanted to know that my kind of love was out there and, that night, just before I kissed Huw I saw my kind of love. I saw it in his eyes – his kindness, his care, his compassion, his *real* beauty. So, I reached out for it. But I knew I couldn't have it.' A half-smile spread from one corner of her mouth. 'It was like being a little girl again. You know, you pick up the toy you really want from off the shelf in the shop. A nice doll maybe. You know it's too expensive, but you want it. You want it so much. But you can't have it. It's there in your hand, but you can't take it out of the box. I don't suppose that makes any sense at all does it?'

'Love rarely makes sense,' replied Maggie.

'Huw loves you,' said Emma. 'Why can't you see that?'

Maggie looked at Emma with a kinder gaze. 'I can see it. I just wanted to hurt him, like he hurt me. It went against everything I stood for as a nurse and a person, and I think I hurt myself just as much as I hurt him.'

Maggie continued to stitch Emma's wound, indeed their discussion had nursed other much older and persistent wounds. All wounds needed to heal, but perhaps the process had started. Time was not an issue.

'Can I say one more thing?' asked Emma.

'Sure.'

'Let him love you, Maggie,' she begged. 'Please, for all our sakes, just let him love you.'

12
Earl Grey and Answers

Autumn was in full swing. The grounds of the cathedral were carpeted with a fusion of crimson, orange, yellow and brown leaves from the late-October trees. As Anwyn took her seat on the bus and looked out of the window to the colourful scene and the symbolism was not lost on her. Like the glorious, yet fragile nature around her, she was staring at the oncoming winter, with all the death and finality that it brings, clean in the face. She didn't relish the drive to the hospital where she would receive news about her memory lapses, so the bus seemed to be the most sensible option. She felt old. She could feel the years in her bones and in her joints and felt certain that her diagnosis would not be a good one. Her short-term memory was still faltering on an almost daily basis.

A couple of stops later, a mother and a young child got on the bus. The mother was quite stocky with a beautiful round face, which seemed to exude kindness. She smiled at Anwyn as she showed her little boy to a seat on the other side of the aisle.

'Nice to be in out of the cold,' she said.

'Yes,' replied Anwyn, 'it certainly is.'

The little boy climbed up and down the seat with excitement, despite his mother's attempts to calm him down a little.

'Look Mummy!' he said. 'We're up really high here! We can look down on all the cars.'

The mother tried to peel him away from the window before turning to Anwyn.

'I'm sorry,' she said. 'He just loves going on the bus. He gets so excited.'

'I can remember being just the same when I was a little girl on the train. I couldn't wait to get on and look out of the window. Are you going somewhere nice today?'

'Just a bit of shopping.' She pulled out a fruit bar and handed it to the little boy in an attempt to distract him from his anticipation. 'You?'

'Hospital,' replied Anwyn.

'Oh, nothing serious, I hope.'

'Just some checks.'

As Anwyn watched the little boy munching away on his confectionery, she was struck by his tenderness and youth. She looked at his little hands, so delicate and weak, and she observed his tiny little feet, struggling to support his body as it jerked around in excitement. She had a real sense of quite how far she had travelled in her body. Age, today, seemed to be calling time on her.

Having negotiated her way through the maze of corridors in the hospital, Anwyn eventually found the waiting room at the neurology unit. Thankfully the waiting room was blessed by a little Bach piano music which pleased Anwyn.

She hated going into the waiting room at the local practice because she loathed the incessant advertisements of the local radio station, with their annoying radio presenters and tendency to play the same songs over and over again. She loved Bach, she loved the elegance of his melodic lines and enjoyed the strange chromatic quirks which offered a sonorous surprise at every turn. Just as *The Well-Tempered Clavier* was beginning to quell her nervousness, a young doctor sporting a fetching waistcoat and meticulously groomed black beard called her. Anwyn rose slowly, hesitated, then followed as though walking to the gallows on a cold, misty morning. He showed her into his office and asked her to take a seat.

'My name is Doctor Mears,' he said with a soft, lulling voice. 'I am the consultant neurologist here and I would like to talk to you about the results of your recent tests.'

Anwyn was frozen. She couldn't acknowledge the doctor, she couldn't nod and her eyes seemed to stare right through him. There were no light-hearted comments, no informalities, just a paralyzing fear which went to the pit of her stomach.

'Are you okay?' Anwyn said nothing, but did manage to somehow convey permission to continue by blinking her eyes and raising her eyebrows slightly. 'We were a little confused with regard to your memory lapses as we could find no sign of any abnormities in any of your scans. They showed no evidence of particular inactivity in any areas of the brain, beyond that which might be expected of a woman of your age.'

Anwyn finally found her voice, 'So, what are you saying? Do you mean there's nothing wrong with me?'

'Well, there certainly isn't any sign of dementia.'

'So I don't have Alzheimer's?'

'No,' said Doctor Mears, 'absolutely not.'

A breeze of relief seemed to flow over Anwyn. The hairs on her arms stood to attention, as if each one had heard the news. Then as the realization set in, her senses suddenly became heightened. Once again, she could smell Michael's aftershave emanating from somewhere within the room. Her head told her that the fragrance came from Doctor Mears, while her heart, now restored, told her that it was Michael. After the pain of the recent months, she allowed herself the luxury of trusting her heart on this occasion. Even through the forming tears in her eyes, she felt as though she could see clearly once again, and in the silent space afforded her by the genial Doctor, her ears caught a sweet refrain of Bach's piano coming from the waiting room outside.

'So what is it?' asked Anwyn gathering herself together. 'The memory loss?'

'Yes,' she replied, 'what's been happening to my mind.'

'Well, I have a theory,' said Doctor Mears, leaning forward over his desk.

'Yes?'

'I contacted your GP to find out a little bit more about you and he told me that you live alone.'

'That's right,' she replied.

'And you have no family.'

'Not really, no.'

Mears straightened his files on his desk. 'He also told me that you lost your husband a while ago.'

'Michael.'

'Yes,' he edged an inch or so closer, 'how have you been?'

'Well, it obviously hasn't been easy.' Anwyn's short-term joy was now being tempered by sadness. 'There's a toothbrush missing from the bathroom, I can make a tin of Earl Grey tea last twice as long and I feel like I have lost a limb at times, but... but I'll make do. What else *can* I do?'

'Who else can you talk to about it?' asked Mears.

'Well...'

'You see, I have hunch that you memory loss is down to depression.'

'Depression?' she exclaimed, 'I'm not a fruit cake you know.'

'No, Mrs Jones,' replied Mears, 'but you are a human being. And you have been through the traumatic process of losing your husband and have no way of dealing with the grief.'

'I'm not sure I really follow.'

'Well, without getting too scientific, there have been some studies in recent years which have made the connection with the reduced function of the hippocampus due to the onset of age, and the short-term impairments on memory function in that area as well as in the prefrontal cortex.'

'English please!'

'In simple terms,' said Mears, 'Depression can cause short-term memory loss.'

'So you think I'm just depressed?'

'There's no such thing as *just* depression. Depression is a very real condition Mrs Jones.' He sat back in his chair, sighed and ran his fingers through his beard. 'It is as real as a broken leg or a dislocated shoulder. Just because you can't see it, doesn't mean it isn't there. It's not a case of being crazy, you're not a loony!' Anwyn raised a smile. 'Mental illness doesn't mean what it used to. We don't lock people up on a whim. It's all different.'

Between the exaltation and confusion, Anwyn started to speak but then stopped. She thought for a moment. Since Michael's death she hadn't had a huge release of emotion. There had been tears but they had fallen in single drops, like drips from the leaking tap in her kitchen. She had yet to experience the deluge of tears, the cataracts of emotions or the longing screams which may or may not constitute "dealing with the grief." She had become friends with Maggie and Huw and, although she had spoken about her past with Michael, she hadn't spoken at any real length about her feelings. This was habit. As a couple, all Anwyn and Michael had was each other. There was never any need to talk to anyone else.

'So what happens now?' she asked.

'I would simply like to try you on some anti-depressant tablets to see if that helps.'

'Do you think it will?'

Mears smiled. 'I'm almost certain it will.' Anwyn put her face in her hands and, in great relief, let out a long sigh. 'But do try and talk to someone as well. If you like we could put you in touch with a counsellor. That might help.'

'No,' said Anwyn rising from her chair, 'I think it's going to be okay.'

Following a day of revelations, Anwyn switched the light on in her open-plan living room and kitchen and fed an excitable Byron a portion of vile-smelling tripe. The little terrier consumed it enthusiastically and even let out a little burp, much to Anwyn's amusement. She switched on the kettle and placed an Earl Grey teabag into a mug. Then she poured the boiling water into the cup and allowed the gentle aroma of bergamot to drift through the air, but as she did so a memory began to stir. It wasn't a particularly poignant memory, it didn't recall some key moment in her life, in fact, she was a little surprised that it was there at all.

She closed her eyes for a moment and found herself lying in bed in her house in London. She was happy. She could hear the sweet but tinny and crackly sound of Bach playing on the gramophone downstairs. The door swung open and in walked Michael carrying a tray with some granary toast and a cup of Earl Grey tea. He placed it on the bed and greeted her with a kiss. Anwyn sat up and placed the tray on her lap. Beneath the cup and saucer was a small folded piece of paper. She unfolded it and read it.

> *To show my love this morn to thee*
> *I offer a cup of Earl Grey tea.*

She giggled, folded it back up and placed it on the tray then told him that it wasn't quite up to his usual standards.

'I've been up all night planning that one out,' he said.

'Ha! Well, you should have started a bit earlier shouldn't you.'

Anwyn took a sip and tasted perfection.

The strengthening wind outside rattled the window and startled her back into the present. She composed herself and carried her drink over to the armchair. Then lowering herself wearily into her seat, she took a sip of her tea. She noted that it didn't taste the way it used to. Nobody made earl grey like Michael. Suddenly a wave crashed over her and she began to feel her loneliness so acutely that it made her heart painful. She could feel pains across her chest and she struggled to regulate her shallow breathing. As the feeling intensified, she felt prickles running up the length of her spine and her scalp began to tingle. The wind outside rattled the door and the windows with incessant ferocity. She could feel her pulse pounding within her, a tympanic pattern which went on and on and on. A simple cup of Earl Grey tea seemed to trigger something in her. She had spent days and nights looking at photographs of Michael. She had heard his voice in her dreams and in her memories, but now something as nugatory as a hot bergamot infusion seemed to unlock the key to her grief. She began to cry. This time however, the tears flowed freely. She howled, she screamed and she wailed with such intensity that Byron made a frightened escape out of the room, cowering with his tail between his little legs. She stood up and in her fury made her way to the kitchen. She opened the cutlery drawers and hurled knives, forks, spoons and a host of other utensils at the wall in a pure rage. Next to suffer her wrath were the cups, saucers and plates, all were smashed on the floor leaving shards of crockery all over the kitchen. Finally, she slumped to the floor and she cried a lifetime of tears in one merciless episode.

One hour later, Anwyn was still sitting on the kitchen floor, her back against the oven. The epilogue to her episode had now rendered her stone-like. Her eyes stared but didn't focus, she heard the wind outside but wasn't listening to anything and her hands, resting on razor-sharp pieces of china, couldn't feel anything. She was numb. Her trance was such that she did not hear the sound of the door being knocked loudly. Her door, unlocked as ever, was pushed open and Maggie walked in. She saw Anwyn slumped against the cooker within a carpet of domestic destruction and made her way over to her.

'Anwyn?' she said softly, frightened of startling her. It was as though she feared waking a sleepwalker from a nightmare. 'Anwyn, what happened here? Are you okay?' she patted Anwyn down checking for injuries. 'Are you hurt? What happened?' Anwyn eventually moved her head toward Maggie and she looked at her with eyes that had never displayed such vulnerability or frailty.

'He's gone.' A lone tear trickled down her face, collected on her top lip and then disappeared into her mouth. 'Michael's gone.'

Maggie ran her fingers through Anwyn's hair. 'Come here, you.' She gathered the old girl up in her arms and held her with all the love she had. 'It'll be okay. I promise.'

After a little while Anwyn managed to escape her stupor and even helped Maggie clear up the mess in the kitchen. Anwyn apologised for not being able to offer her friend a cup of tea as most of the receptacles were smashed to smithereens. She tried to explain what had happened, but couldn't. Later, after Maggie had left, promising to return in the morning, Anwyn tried to explain to herself what had happened. How could something as trivial as a cup of tea trigger so much emotion? Perhaps, she wondered, it was the last straw after months of emotional erosion. Whatever it was, it had been agonising, but as the furious night-time fell, she began to feel some clarity. She could sense her own storm abating and tiny rays of sunshine illuminating her with hope. That night, as she sat up in bed in her quiet, crepuscular room, she felt compelled to write a verse about her feelings. It always seemed to work for Michael. She pulled out a notebook from her bedside table and began to

147

write beneath a weak lamplight.

Earl Grey

It's not when <u>that</u> day comes around.
I just surround my fragile self with sound,
And I lose the din of you slowly dying
And the echoes of my emptiness crying.
It's not when another Christmas comes along
With merriment and hearty song,
That I must smile on through
And contemplate another year, a lifetime without you.
It's not when the wedding bells chime
And I see the bride and groom kiss, I'm
Reminded of our carnal embrace,
Then my final view of your face.
I can even cope when your birthday arrives,
And only a fading memory survives,
Un-drawing your picture from my mind,
Leaving only faint outlines behind.
But in the morning I can't make my tea
The way you used to make it for me.
As the water fountains from the kettle
My tears fall into the Earl Grey and settle.
Then the grief accosts me again
And sings her cruel refrain.

She knew the poem was far from perfect, but as she read aloud to herself, she felt something she had not felt within her for a long time; peace. With that she turned out the light and called Byron up on to the bed. He leapt up and wagged his tail.

'Give me a cuddle, Byron.'

13
The Storm

The postman called early that day. Usually letters would not be delivered until lunchtime at the earliest, but a collection of commercial flotsam and bills landed at the foot of the front door just before a quarter-to-nine. Peter, still suspended from school, filed through the post and tucked between a leaflet for a local Indian take-a-way and a letter requesting financial support from the Red Cross, he found a white envelope stamped with the coat of arms of the Pembrokeshire magistrates. It was addressed to his parents; however, his eagerness to find out more pertaining to the case against him meant that Peter's curiosity got the better of him. In the absence of his mother and father, who had both left for work, he opened the letter and read it out loud.

A hearing had been arranged for three weeks' time. All of a sudden everything was very real. The recent weeks had been spent in the comfort of his own home. Ironically, his grades during that time had improved greatly. He had no need to worry about the sarcastic comments of others, no need to concern himself with the indifference of the teachers to his predicament and, most importantly, he didn't have to worry about the daily beatings, trips in the corridor or fishing his PE kit out of the urinals in the boys changing room. He wanted to continue this way. For Peter, education, like everything else in his life, worked best when there were no others around to screw it up.

Having done all of the school work set for him by eleven o'clock in the morning, Peter spent the rest of the day at the beach, collecting shells and searching for fossils, as well as picking up and examining various forms of marine life from the little rock pools. After that, he made his way to Darwin's grave. He sat there for a couple of hours, just talking. He told Darwin about the letter regarding his case, his fears about going back to school and discussed with him the emerging idea that he would be better taught at home. He wondered how his parents would react to the notion that he wouldn't go back to the school. Every now and then, he would look out over the waves and see the lighthouse standing stoically in the strengthening seas. In the fading light it would send delicate illuminations flashing toward the shore. Once again, it seemed to be calling to him, beckoning him to the pleasures of solitude, to a life of simplicity and therefore, happiness.

Later that evening at the dinner table, Huw, Maggie and Peter were doing their best to engage in small talk, as if trying to rebuild their relationships word by word. In a true British style they discussed the weather (always an interesting subject on the west coast of Wales), before moving on to a laboured debate about the evening's television choices. Smiles were strained, laughter felt manufactured rather than natural but at least they were evident. In the pauses between comments, one could easily imagine the cogs in everybody's brain grinding away, thinking of how to fill each moment of silent awkwardness – but at least they were trying. Although they were small steps, they were at least going in the right direction. Peter recognised this and decided to approach the subject of school.

'Can I ask you both a question?' he said.

'What is it?' replied Huw.

'I have been thinking about school.' He put down his knife and fork.

'What about it?'

Peter took in a deep breath and went for broke. 'I don't want to go back.'

Maggie laughed. 'What do you mean? You have to go back, it's the law.'

'I'm not saying I don't want to study, but I don't want to go back to *that* school.'

Huw scratched his head. 'Well, there are no other schools around here, not unless you are willing to get on a bus and travel a lot.'

'No,' replied Peter, 'I mean I want to study from home. I want to be home-schooled.'

'Why?' asked Maggie

'Why do you think?'

'Look,' said Huw, 'I know you have had it rough there for a while…'

'Rough? They beat me up, Dad. Day after day after day.'

'But running away isn't going to solve the matter,' said Huw.

'So what do I do?' asked Peter. 'The last time I didn't run away I got suspended.'

Maggie intervened. 'There is a difference between not running away and breaking somebody's nose.'

'And why did I do that?'

'You tell us,' replied Maggie.

'Because there are only so many times you can beg for mercy. Because there are only so many times you can run. And if you do run, they chase you until they find you. All that Sunday School crap about offering the other cheek… That's not how it works. Not at that school.'

'But who would teach you?'

'You guys,' he said.

'I wouldn't know the first thing about teaching,' replied Maggie.

'We both have jobs, you know,' said Huw.

'We can't just give up everything just because you don't want to go to school.'

'It's not just about not wanting to go to school,' Peter replied angrily. 'Since I have been at home I have produced really good work and my grades are improving. I actually enjoy school… when I'm not there.'

'You don't just go to school for the education,' said Maggie softly, trying to calm the situation down a little, 'there's the social aspect too.'

'Your Mother's right,' affirmed Huw. 'You're not going to make friends if you are stuck in the house all day.'

'That's fine by me.'

'Oh, don't be so naïve, Peter,' snapped Huw. 'What are you going to do? Become a hermit? You need people around you.'

'People let you down!' said Peter. 'They always have and

they always will. Why can't you understand that I am *happy* on my own?'

A long awkwardness ensued. Huw and Maggie looked at each other, both looking to the other to speak.

'I'm sorry, Peter,' said Huw, finally. 'It's just not possible.'

'What if we had a tutor come to the house?' pleaded Peter.

'And who is going to pay for it?' snapped Huw.

'I don't know.' Peter bowed his head.

'I'm sorry, Peter.' Huw stretched out his hand only to have it declined sharply. 'It just can't be done.'

Peter stood up, tucked his chair beneath the table and took his plate to the sink. Before leaving he turned back to his parents for one last comment.

'I'm *not* going back to that school.'

Peter said nothing more to his parents that night. When Maggie opened his door at half-past-ten to tell him to turn out the light, he pretended to be asleep so he wouldn't have to converse. He was angry and scared. He had spent the entire evening weeping silently beneath his covers. By the time his digital wristwatch beeped at eleven o'clock, wearied by his tears, he had fallen into a deep sleep.

A rumble began. The light that appeared through the cracks of the bedroom door went out and the room began to feel cold. Outside the window, a large blood-red moon rose above the lighthouse. The rain began to fall outside, soft at first, then in fast-moving, sidewinding sheets. Peter, lying on his side in his bed, the sheets pulled up to his ears, opened his eyes and watched the door creep open. A hand reached around the door and pushed it open slowly. A dark figure, faceless and dressed in a school blazer came and sat at the end of his bed. It was followed by another, before his bedroom window opened proceeded by an icy blast of the westerly wind. Another dark figure climbed in through the window, again with no facial features, and sat in the corner of his room. The figures kept coming into the room, crowding the space until Peter couldn't see the window or the door. Then, through the crowd of anonymous gatherers, two familiar faces entered. Kelly Moore and Adam Bargewood emerged with iniquitous smiles, the latter still with blood dripping from his nose. In the darkness they shone torches into Peter's eyes. Suddenly Peter could not move. The dream rendered him paralysed as Moore removed a tin pencil case from his pocket and handed it to Bargewood. The case was opened slowly revealing a collection of feathers, beneath which was a stationery compass which Bargewood picked out. He stared at its needle-sharp point and grinned. Moore took hold of Peter's arm and held it outside the bed. A terrified Peter tried to pull his arm away to no avail. His body wriggled and writhed but his arm was completely still. Without saying a word, Bargewood leaned in and placed the point of the compass on Peter's thin, pale arm. His breathing became more and more rapid and his pulse stormed through his brain mercilessly. Bargewood began to carve into his flesh with the compass. As the skin opened up and the blood began to ooze out, Peter began to scream and plead, much to the vile laughter of Bargewood and Moore. The pain was relentless and as the gathered figures moved in closer, Peter saw the words *SEE YOU SOON NATURE BOY!* carved into his skin. As he looked at the seeping wound, to his horror, he saw a single maggot wriggling and writhing toward the surface. He began to feel nauseous, the smell of vomit rising through his nostrils. He screamed at the top of his shrill voice, the din disturbed him from his slumber. In the darkness of the empty room he sat up, breathing heavily, his pulse charging through his veins like a stampede. He wiped away the perspiration of his nightmare from his brow, stood up and made his way nervously to the bedroom door. With his hand trembling, he edged it open slowly and saw the corridor outside; nothing out of the ordinary. It had been a dream but how portentous was it? Peter spent the next hour pacing up and down his room trying to shake the dream from his mind, yet he couldn't lose the image of his tormentor's face. Peter came to the conclusion that St David's offered him little more than a continuance of his nightmare and if his parents refused to take his concerns seriously, there was only one course of action he could take – leave.

Drawers were raided and their contents hurled into a backpack. Jumpers, shirts, socks and underwear were unceremoniously forced into the bag, although the school uniform, the symbol of his agony, was pushed deep into his wastebasket. Peter said goodbye to Terry and tried to assure him that he would be taken care of.

'I'm not coming back,' he said, looking at the spider hiding in the corner of his little glass box. 'I'm sorry, but if I don't go now, I never will.'

Peter looked at the picture of the lighthouse on his wall and nodded to himself. He picked up his raincoat, heaved his backpack onto his shoulder and took a last look at his bedroom. Finally, with a memory of his mother reading him a story in the very same room running through his head, he took a deep breath and walked out.

Creaking floorboards seemed to accompany every step as Peter edged downstairs, passing the grandfather clock at the bottom which tick-tocked ever closer to five o'clock. He felt sure that his movements would disturb his parent's sleep, but somehow he managed to move surreptitiously down the hallway toward the front door. On his way he passed the key rack and delicately picked up his father's boat keys. He had spent many a day watching his father start up the boat and head out on a dolphin tour, now it would be his escape to… to a quieter life. He walked out of the front door, deciding not to close it fully so as not to wake his parents, and then, finally, left home.

By the time he reached the boat launch, the light from the dawning sun was beginning to creep over the horizon to the east. The wind was picking up and moving in quickly from the remnants of the dark west. As Peter threw his backpack aboard his father's boat, he looked at the waters of the bay and saw how choppy they were. He knew that choppy waters in the bay meant that the conditions at open sea would be tumultuous to say the least. As the little boat rocked, Peter jumped aboard and lost his footing. He slipped with a squeak of his sneakers, fell backwards and thumped his head hard on a passenger chair. He yelled. As he made his way up to his feet again, he rubbed his head and realized that he had cut it. Although hardly a gushing, gaping wound, it was certainly not the start to his journey that he had been hoping for. He released the boat from its moorings, put the keys in the ignition and started the engine. It was six o'clock in the morning, the cormorants were calling, the gulls were soaring in the sky above, and Peter was on his way.

Anwyn had woken early that morning. She awoke at five feeling renewed and headed out early with Byron down to her boat for a walk and to continue some of the final renovations on the boat. The boat, now in full working order, was still a couple of licks of paint short of perfection but, like rest of life following her positive news from the doctor, almost restored. The light was softly illuminating the bay and Byron and Anwyn watched the early morning terns coasting over the waters. Wanting to follow them a little more closely, Anwyn picked out her binoculars and followed the birds across the skyline, high, low and wide. As she scanned downwards she spotted Huw's boat speeding out of the bay with Peter at the helm.

'What the bloody hell is he doing, Byron?' asked an incredulous Anwyn. 'Where's he going?'

With no mobile phone, no working CB radio on the boat, and the prospect of running back up the cliff to the house to raise an alarm on her landline not worthy of entertaining, Anwyn only had one option. She had to follow Peter. The boat had yet to take to the waves and Anwyn could not have foreseen a maiden voyage under such circumstances, however she felt she had no choice.

She called to Byron, gathered him in her arms and climbed aboard her vessel. Anticipating an unsteady voyage she picked up Byron and placed him in a chest fixed into the side of the boat near the helm, so that he would not be hurled about while she negotiated the wild waters. She removed the mooring and headed out into the bay.

The choppy waters of the bay crashed into the bow of Anwyn's little boat sending surf crashing into her windows. She struggled to keep sight of Peter in the distance and so increased her speed to get as close to him as possible. The fear in her heart was tangible. She had experience skippering boats, but that was over thirty years ago and certainly not in these conditions. Every now and then she would check the chest to see that Byron was okay, before continuing to yo-yo across the waves.

In front of Anwyn, Peter continued heading toward the lighthouse. As he travelled, a pod of dolphins swam either side of him, guiding him and protecting him as best they could. Peter could hear two conflicting voices within him; the first, his heart, was telling him to keep going, to continue through the uncertainty of the western waters, for it was better than certain agonies which awaited back at the school; the second was his head, telling him to return to the shore, to go home, to hold his parents like he had never held them before, to tell them that he loved them, in the belief that they would do the right thing and take him out of the school once and for all.

As Anwyn followed, making up the distance on Peter minute by minute, the waves of the open sea began to rise. As a large wave crashed into the boat she lost her footing and almost fell, however her grip on the helm was so strong that she somehow managed to maintain her balance. The sea water was beginning to drench the floor of the boat making it slippery and even harder to stand.

Peter looked into the distance and saw the lighthouse drawing closer. As he bobbed up and down it seemed to dip in and out of the waves and move from left to right. Then, in front of him he saw a huge wave approaching him. His heart leapt as he considered how best to negotiate it. There was no way that he could move around the wave in time and there was certainly not enough time to about turn.

There was only one option; take the hit. As the wave neared he cowered down with hands still at the controls of the boat while the foreboding panic surged through his body. With the wave but metres away he closed his eyes and held on with all his strength. Eventually the wave consumed him, covering him with icy waters as the boat was tossed into the air like a toy. On returning to the waves with a violent crash, Peter was thrown forward into the control panel, thumping his head once more, resulting in yet another cut, this time just above his left eyebrow. As he regained his footing he saw that his backpack was gone. He looked around the boat to no avail and then to his horror he noticed it being carried away on the crest of a disappearing wave.

Watching from two hundred meters away, Anwyn winced as she saw Peter being thrown around the waves. She increased the power on the boat and sped up toward the boy.

As Peter neared the island, he spied the docking area but struggled in the waves to reach it. Bookending the short area of levelled concrete and the two large mooring bollards was a large area of sharp, jagged rocks which protruded inauspiciously into the freezing waves. Peter fought to maintain his footing while he tried to lasso his rope over the bollard. He struggled wearily from left to right. After a number of failed attempts to fix his rope, another larger wave ploughed him into the rocks to the sound of a large crash. As the tide pulled him back out to sea, Peter noticed that water was coming in through a large hole at the stern. It was only a matter of time before the boat would sink.

As Peter struggled to moor the boat to the dock before it sank completely, he saw Anwyn's boat approaching.

'Help!' he cried.

'Just hang on Peter!' ordered Anwyn. 'I'm coming for you now.'

Peter, in his panic, made one more attempt to reach the bollard with his rope, but as he did so the vessel was struck by another huge wave. It tipped the boat sharply on the port side, sending Peter crashing into the glacial water. As he descended beneath the waves the world seemed peaceful and, for a moment, he considered breathing in deeply, taking death into his young lungs and letting everything slip away. However, the waves which could force him down to the bottom of the ocean, could also drag him to the surface. He emerged from the waves and inhaled sharply and saw Anwyn's boat closing in. The weight of his clothes and shoes made treading water a Sisyphean task, while the biting temperatures rendered his muscles useless.

Anwyn came within twenty feet or so and called Peter, 'Here, catch!'

She hurled an inflatable ring toward Peter and told him to swim toward it. Peter flailed his arms wildly in an attempt to reach the ring, but while each hurried stroke would propel him forward one metre, the indeterminate waves seemed to pull him three metres away. Finally, fortune favoured him and sent him crashing into the ring, which he managed to take hold of. He held on to the rope around the ring which now tethered him safely to Anwyn's boat, and began to pull himself in. Anwyn pulled him from the boat and eventually she reached Peter and pulled him aboard, his soaking clothes clinging tightly to his body. Between them both they managed to find the relative safety of Anwyn's boat. Peter sat down, shivering and struggling to catch his breath while Anwyn neared the boat to the dock. A brief respite in the ferocity of the waves allowed her to reach close enough to the dock to secure the moorings. Anwyn picked out some spare blankets from a hold in the boat and threw her first aid kit ashore. Finally, she lifted Byron in her arms and along with a dripping wet Peter, stepped on solid ground.

The entrance to the lighthouse lay at the top of a steep escarpment of steps. Peter wrung as much sea water out of his clothes as he could and climbed up the steps with a bedraggled Anwyn and Byron following on behind. Upon reaching the tatty wooden door, complete with peeling shavings of white paint, they found that it swung open quite easily. The two made it inside and shut the door behind them to escape the westerly winds and the first spots of precipitation.

'Right,' said Anwyn, 'take off your clothes, before you freeze.'

Peter undressed slowly and awkwardly. His teeth chattered an allegro rhythm as he mumbled an apology while Anwyn placed the blankets around his naked shoulders. She squeezed some more water out of his clothes and spread them out over the rail of a spiral staircase, which lead to the control room at the top of the lighthouse.

'Come on,' she said, 'let's get upstairs. You lead on, I might take a while with these old legs of mine. See if there is anyone there.'

'There won't be anyone in here,' replied Peter, his quivering voice echoing up the spiral staircase.

'Why not?' asked Anwyn

'Because all the lighthouses are run b-b-by computer.'

'What?' Anwyn exclaimed. 'You mean there's no rough-faced, bearded man in a big woolly jumper and smoking a pipe up there?'

'No,' he replied, 'j-j-just a computer.'

'Bugger!' She stopped to catch her breath, 'I thought my luck was in for a moment.'

On their laborious ascent, they came upon three empty rooms, adorned only by a window and a staircase leading up to more uninteresting rooms. They finally arrived at the top of the lighthouse and entered a large, circular control room. Pointing to the west stood a control panel, with a number of buttons which meant nothing to either of them. However, at one end of the console there stood an old-fashioned red telephone, complete with traditional springy coiled lead. An auspicious sign beneath it read, EMERGENCY!

'Thank goodness for that,' said Anwyn. She picked up the phone and waited for a tone. Nothing.

'What's wrong?' asked Peter, shuddering in the cold.

'It's dead,' she replied. 'Still, nice view from here though.'

'So nobody knows we're here?'

'That's right,' said Anwyn, 'and I don't think I have enough fuel to get back. It was something of an unscheduled journey you called me out on.'

'*I* didn't call you out.'

'Well, I could hardly have let you go out alone, could I?'

'I'd have been okay,'

'Oh, really!' she said sarcastically. 'Were you planning to swim the rest of the way?' Peter rolled his eyes. 'Where were you going anyway?'

'What does it matter?'

'It matters.'

Peter began to shiver a little harder. Anwyn pulled him close. They sat down on the floor beneath the control panel and huddled together for warmth. She called Byron.

'Come on, you little bugger,' she said playfully, 'huddle up and cuddle up.' Peter offered a hint of a smile. 'He's my little hot water bottle. When it's cold at night, he snuggles up in the bed with me. It's surprising how much heat he can produce, particularly if I feed him tripe!'

Peter stroked Byron behind the ear as the little dog nuzzled into him. Within a few minutes Byron's eyes had almost closed. Clearly the adventure had been particularly trying for him.

'Dad's going to kill me.'

'I'm sure he'll be relieved to see you're okay,' said Anwyn, rubbing Peter's arms to produce little warmth.

'No, he won't be worried about me, but when he sees his boat…'

'Well, that's what insurance is for! I wouldn't worry about that, now. You've probably done him a favour, he'll be able to get another one, a better one.'

Peter shook his head, 'I'm not sure about that.'

'Come one,' her voice softened, 'what's all this really about?'

'They want me to go back to the school.'

'And you don't want to go back?'

'Why?' he asked. 'So they can beat me up again?'

'From what I heard, I can't imagine you'll be bothered by them ever again. I hear you gave them a taste of their own medicine.'

'You don't understand,' suddenly his face seemed a little paler, weaker. 'They'll *never* stop. Even if they never hit me again, there's all of the things they say.'

'Sticks and stones…' began Anwyn.

'Don't say that, please! The words are just as bad, sometimes worse.'

Anwyn apologised, 'I didn't mean to make light of… That was silly of me. I, more than most, should know about the power of words. My husband made a living out of powerful words, but they were usually used for good. He used them to express things which were beautiful, rather than hate.'

Peter sniffed. 'What was your husband like?'

Anwyn thought for a while. 'You know, he was actually like you.'

'Me!' exclaimed Peter.

'Yes, you!'

'In what way?' asked Peter. 'Was he a weirdo too?'

Anwyn gave him a little scornful look. Peter apologised. 'He was different. But that's what made him so interesting. He was unpredictable, some might say tempestuous at times. He had a real temper. But then he had a tenderness like no other. He wasn't interested in the things that most people concerned themselves with. We didn't have a TV, we never had the interweb, never had those wretched mobile phone things…'

Peter interjected. 'Why?'

'Because they are just *things*,' she replied. 'They get in the way of the things that matter; love, friendship and compassion. Michael and I talked more in one evening than some couples do in a lifetime. They're too busy watching crap on the telly or with their eyes glued to a phone. That's not living, that's existing.' Peter nodded.

'What did you talk about?' asked Peter.

'Everything!'

Peter persisted. 'Such as?'

'Oh, we talked about religion - that could go on for days. I think we managed to disprove almost every major religion. He always had a soft spot for Buddhism, though. He said it was the only *useful* religion out there and that monotheism was truly dangerous.'

'Monotheism?' Peter enquired.

'Religions with one God.'

'I don't believe in God,' said Peter, a wave of coldness shuddering over him.

'I shouldn't say this,' said Anwyn, 'what with you being at a Christian school, but I think you have come to a wise decision.'

'I mean, it's one rule for one and one for another isn't it?'

'Go on,' said Anwyn.

'Well, in the ten commandments God tells us we shouldn't kill, then he kills all of those children in Egypt, just to teach the pharaoh a lesson. Then he asked Abraham to kill his son, just to test his love. What kind of God would do that?'

'I don't know,' replied Anwyn, pulling him in a little closer.'

'The same kind of God that puts people on earth who... their only reason for being here is to make other people's lives agony.'

'Are you talking about the boys that you beat up?'

'I had to. If I hadn't I would have...' he hesitated.

'Go on,' said Anwyn, softly encouraging him. 'What would you have done?'

Peter turned his head and caught Anwyn's eye, as if looking for someone in her gaze that he could trust. He inhaled deeply then sighed heavily.

'One day, about a year ago, we had a PE lesson. I hate them. I've never been very good at any sports. I can't stand sports.' He shook his head a little, 'But that's not why I hate them. I hate them because in the changing rooms the teacher is never there, so they can do anything… and they did. In the changing rooms they used to… to play tricks… do things to me. They used to put my clothes in the urinal, piss all over them, then make me put them on. They used to whip me with soaking wet towels and leave marks all over my body. Anyway, that day we had PE straight after break, so I went in to get changed before the session started, I thought I'd be able to get changed before they came in. But they followed me in and it was worse because there was no one to see anything, no witnesses. They hit me but, by that time I was beginning to get used to the beatings, I mean they hurt, but I could kind of shut it out. It was a bit like… like being unconscious. But after they beat me up…' Peter's voice quivered, '…after they beat me up… they pushed me into the long, steel urinal, they both pissed on me. They fucking pissed on me, all over my clothes. I couldn't move. I *didn't* move. I just… just let it happen. When the class came in for PE, they just laughed. When they all went out on to the field, I put my PE kit on, at least that was clean, and ran out of the school, stealing a school tie on the way. I didn't know why I took the tie, it just kind of happened, like it was… automatic. I ran down to the park and just sat there. It was freezing, just like now. Then …something took over me. I don't know what it was, I don't know where it came from. I wasn't thinking, I was just… I was just *doing*. I climbed up on the first branch, about ten feet up, I wrapped the tie around my throat and tied the other end to the branch and then I fell. The branch snapped. There was a horrible pain in my neck, I landed on my back and I cracked my head on the floor. I was in so much pain… but it was *nothing* compared to the pain in my mind.' Peter began to cry. But it was a welcome cry. It was warm wave of relief. His steamy tears brought a little heat to his cold face and fell on him like warm summer rain.

'Why didn't you tell anyone?' asked Anwyn planting a soft kiss on Peter's head.

'Who could I tell?' he sniffed. 'The teachers at school thought I was weird too. Mum and Dad were… well, they had enough on their plates. So I used to tell the animals. I told Terry, I used to talk to the stick insects and my hamster. And then I found Darwin on the beach one day. For the first time in my life I felt like I had some power. When I picked him up, when I held him in my hands, I realised that I had real power in *my* hands. I could have crushed him, I could have treated him the same way that Kelly Moore and Adam Bargewood treated me. But I also had the power to help him. I had the power to look after him, the power to… to love him. But I soon realized that I needed him more than he needed me. I told him everything, I told him about my day, my dreams, my fears. He gave me a reason to live.'

'I understand.'

'So when they killed him…' he hesitated, '…it felt like they killed me too. It was like I had nothing to lose.'

'Have you told you parents what you are telling me?'

'No,' said Peter, 'of course not.'

'You need to tell them,'

'I can't they're going through enough as it is, Mum's always busy, Dad's struggling with his business, although they think I don't know about that. They're too busy.'

'They're not too busy to love you,' said Anwyn. Peter bowed his head and allowed another tear to fall. 'You need to talk to them, tell them what you told me. It's the only way they will *really* understand.'

Peter nodded. He knew she was right, but he also knew that telling his parents about his attempts to take his own life, would take far more courage than he needed to floor Bargewood and Moore. He wondered if they would be angry that he had not told them. Would they feel guilty that they had not truly understood the extent to his loneliness? Or would they be happy that everything was in the open?

'Right,' said Anwyn. 'Let's have a look at all these buttons. One of them must be able to get us out of here.'

Anwyn stood up, with a little help from Peter, and made her way to the mystery that was the lighthouse console. Buttons flashed, beeped and pipped, and terms like *auxiliary* and *rotary* created yet more confusion. A small screen on the console read, 'function normal'.

'One of these buttons should do *something*,' said Anwyn. 'What about this one?' She pushed a large red button, but nothing happened. Once again Anwyn tried the phone but to no avail. 'Still dead,' she said.

Peter got to his feet, wrapped the blanket around him and made his way to the console to help.

'What about this one?' he said pressing a yellow button a number of times.

Anwyn chuckled. 'I don't bloody well know! I can't even work the radio properly. I'm practically Amish!' Anwyn and Peter laughed and looked at each other, this time as true friends. Despite the generational differences, a connection had been made and a bond of trust and love now existed.

The laughter escalated to a raucous symphony of joy between them as they began to press every button in sight. When nothing happened they began to palm multiple buttons at once, and Peter even jumped on the console and began to press the buttons with his feet, much to the hilarity of Anwyn. Just as she was catching her breath between waves of laughter, Peter began to sit on the console and effect the controls with his buttocks. Anwyn erupted once more and revelled in the sight of Peter doing something she had never seen him do; smile. As he continued his exuberance, Anwyn paused for a moment and watched Peter playing on the console. After a minute or so Peter stopped to see his friend watching him, a warm smile adorning her face.

'What is it?' asked Peter.

'Oh, nothing.'

Peter climbed down off the console, 'Come on. What are you smiling at?'

'It's just…'

Peter persisted. 'What?'

'It's just, while you were dancing up there, I saw you as a child for the first time.'

'Oh, sorry,' said Peter.

'Don't apologise,' smiled Anwyn, 'I get the feeling you have had to grow up a little too soon. There's nothing wrong with being a child. Enjoy it. Be a child for as long as you can.'

Peter smiled softly.

The smell of burned toast drifted through the house having just set off the fire alarm. Huw guzzled down his last dregs of morning coffee and searched for his keys.

'Have you seen them?' he asked

'Seen what?'

'My keys.'

'No, sorry,' replied Maggie. 'I'll ask Peter.

As Huw continued to look high and low for his keys, Maggie stood at the bottom of the stairs calling Peter's name to increasing consternation. Huw, who while searching for his keys, was putting his warm winter coat on, ready for another day at sea, called as well. They looked at each other, perplexed.

'He's usually up and dressed by now,' said Maggie.

'I know,' replied Huw. 'Hang on, I'll go and wake him.'

Huw heavy-footed his way up the stairs and tapped on his son's door.

'Peter?' No response. 'Peter, come on! You can't stay in there all day. Look, I know you're angry, I know you're upset, but hiding away in there all day isn't going to do anyone any good.' Silence. 'Peter!'

Finally, Huw pushed the door open and saw that Peter was gone. 'Oh, shit!' he cursed. He saw an open cupboard and could see that many of his clothes had disappeared. He rummaged hurriedly through the drawers and saw an absence of socks and underwear. He cursed again.

'What's wrong?' asked Maggie from the foot of the stairs.

'He's gone!' exclaimed Huw.

'What do you mean he's gone?'

'I mean *he's gone*! He's taken his clothes and disappeared.'

'Oh my God, no!' Maggie's stance became less assured and she held on to the bannister for support. 'Not my boy.'

Huw could see the horror in Maggie's eyes and tried to settle her as she became more and more agitated. She started to shake as the tears started to stream down her face.

'It's okay,' he said, 'I'll call the police. We'll have him back soon.'

'What if he's gone for good?' Maggie struggled to control her breathing as her crying became more hysterical. 'What if we never see him again? I can't lose him. I can't.'

'We *won't* lose him!'

'How do you know? What makes you so sure?'

'I'm his Dad,' said Huw, 'I *have* to be sure.'

Just at that moment the phone rang and startled them both.

'It might be Peter,' said Huw. He picked up the phone before it had barely had chance for a second ring. 'Hello!'

'Hi, it's me,' said Emma's voice on a crackly line. 'Where is your boat?'

'What do you mean?' asked Huw.

'It's not here,' replied Emma. 'I've just come out to get things ready for the first trip out; I have two Japanese tourists with a multitude of cameras around their necks waiting where the boat should be and no boat! Is it moored up somewhere else?'

'Hang on a minute, Emma!' Huw dropped the phone on the stairs and double-checked the key rack and realized why his boat keys were missing. 'Oh, my God!'

'What is it?' asked Maggie urgently.

'He's taken my boat.' He picked up the phone once again. 'Emma, I'll call you back. Peter has taken the boat.'

'Peter?'

'Yes,' he said, 'he's gone and it looks like he's taken my boat.'

'But why would he…'

Huw interrupted, '…I can't explain now, but can you cancel all trips for today and keep an eye out for Peter in case he comes back to the launch?'

'Yes, of course,' replied Emma.

Huw hung up and dialled the emergency services. 'Hello, I think I need the coastguard.'

Anwyn and Peter stood looking out of the lighthouse window. They walked the perimeter of the room taking in the three-hundred-and-sixty degree views of the world outside. Peter, still with the blanket wrapped around him, looked out and was mesmerised by the beauty of the open sea. Outside, the wind was beginning to blow, rattling the windows of the lighthouse with ghostly cries and calls.

'So where were you heading?' asked Anwyn.

'Sorry?' replied Peter, startled from his reverie.

'You must have been going somewhere, but where?'

'Here.'

'What on earth would you want to come here for?'

Peter stepped a little closer to the windowpane. 'Look, what do you see out there?'

'What is this, Peter?' asked Anwyn with mischief in her voice. 'If it's eye-spy and the letter is 's' I think I'll get it in two.'

'No,' said Peter, 'look! No people. Not a soul.'

'Anwyn's voice became a little more delicate. 'And you like that?'

'Why *wouldn't* you like that? It's people who screw things up. The things they say, the things they do… the things they don't do.'

'Well, I hate to tell you Peter,' said Anwyn, 'but that includes you too.'

'What's that supposed to mean?'

'None of us are perfect, Peter. You have said things, done things and not done things too. You took your father's boat and risked your life. Just imagine how your parents are feeling now.'

'They're probably glad to be rid of me.'

'I don't believe that for a second,' she placed her hand on his shoulder, 'and I don't think you do either. We're not perfect, but that doesn't mean you should just give up on everyone. Take us for example. We're sitting here talking like friends, because we are friends. But I bet you thought I was a miserable old cow when you first met me.' Peter said nothing. 'Thank you for your honesty. But here we are, talking, and you have told me things that you haven't told anyone else in the world. Are you going to give up on me too?'

'You're different,' reasoned Peter.

'*Everyone* is different,' asserted Anwyn. 'But that's what makes things interesting. You and I are very different and yet we are friends. I mean, you are young and handsome, while I am an ugly old cow whose ear hair is accelerating at an alarming rate and for no good reason.' Peter chuckled. 'You are clearly a very clever young man, while I can't even work the sodding toaster.'

'We do have one thing in common,' said Peter once his laughter had subsided.

'What's that?' asked Anwyn, rubbing the tops of his arms to keep him warm.

'We're both lonely.'

Anwyn was taken aback at the level of the boy's insight into her personality. She offered a sad smile. 'Yes, I suppose so.' Anwyn thought for a moment. She stepped away and wandered to the other side of the lighthouse. She folded her arms and looked up to the gathering clouds in the west. 'Do you mind if I tell you something, Peter?'

'No, what?'

'I had a problem with my memory.'

'What kind of problem?'

'I was beginning to forget silly things, like leaving the tap running, or boiling the kettle when it had already boiled. But then I forgot my own husband's name once and I thought I was going mad. I thought I was losing my mind. You see Michael and I, we weren't particularly materialistic. We never had a television, never had computers or mobile phones, never needed electric kettles or an automatic this, that or the other. The house was never cluttered up with anything other than books. We used to read all the time. When we weren't reading, we were talking. You see all that other crap, all those *things*, they never distracted us from each other from the love we had. These days, lovers, if that is what they really are, can be in the same room, or even the same bed, and yet be in another world. People are looking for the world in the palm of their hand. I see them searching all the time, tapping the little screens, looking for the world. That's not the world, not the *real* world. You find that in the people you love, the places you love. And you create a world with memories, your mind, your thoughts. And the great thing is, is that you don't need to get a newer, better model all of the time because the more you use that mind, the more you build your memories, the better it becomes. It improves with age. That is until the day when you start to forget things. And then you realise you can't just buy a new model, there *is* no new model. There is nothing that can replace a lifetime of memories. I thought I was going to lose Michael all over again. I dreaded the day that I picked up his photo and wondered who he was. I thought I was going mad.'

'Were you?' asked Peter, talking to her back.

'Well it was a problem with my mind,' she replied. 'But it wasn't my memory.'

'What was it?'

Anwyn turned to Peter, at first her head to the floor, then with determination, looking straight into his eyes. 'Black bile, my boy! Black bile.'

'What's that?' looking a little squeamish.

'Meloncholia, the black dog, the blues.' Peter still looked confused. 'Depression.'

'Oh!' said Peter. 'So that made you lose your memories?'

'Nearly,' replied Anwyn. 'I thought I might lose everything.'

'But you're okay now, aren't you?'

'I think…' she swallowed. A tear was permitted to fall from, her eye. '…I think I'm going to be fine. I just had to realise that there was no shame in loving him that much, no shame in missing him as much as I do, no shame in wanting to hold him. In fact, I realised that the level of my grief was equal to the level of my love for him… and his love for me. I just … I allowed myself to grieve. It's not a weakness, it's not selfish, it's not self-indulgent or moping around, it's just what we do. It's what we have done for thousands of years to cope with *real* loss.'

Peter smiled, 'So, what do you do now?'

'I live.' Another tear drifted down through the lines in her face, negotiating a growing smile on its way to her chin. 'I carry on loving him, that doesn't change. *Death Shall Have no Dominion.*'

'What's that?' asked Peter

'Dylan Thomas,' replied Anwyn.

'Who?' asked Peter innocently.

'What do you mean, who? Call yourself a Welshman? You should be ashamed of yourself young man!' Peter laughed. 'There is one other thing we need to do, though.'

'What's that?'

'We need to get out of here!'

Peter gave a cheeky grin. 'Yes, but how? It's all automated.'

Anwyn looked bemused. 'English please!'

'I mean it's probably operated from the mainland. They probably keep it going and just operate the controls from somewhere else. That's probably why we couldn't change it by pressing any of those buttons.'

'So someone on the mainland just... checks that it's working, checks that it's on?'

Peter shrugged his shoulders. 'I don't know. I'm just guessing.'

Anwyn walked over to the console and surveyed all of the baffling technology. 'So, if they found out there was a problem, they would send someone out to investigate. Wouldn't they?'

'Why? What are you are you going to do?' asked a rather apprehensive Peter.

A sly grin spread across Anwyn's face. 'We're going to play a little game.'

'What kind of game?' he asked suspiciously

'It's called, *pull the wire.*'

'What?'

'You heard me,' she said. 'Now look for some wires and start pulling them out.'

'You are joking.'

'No I'm bloody-well not!' Anwyn began to search around the console. 'If we can bugger up all of these blibs and blobs, then hopefully someone will come and sort it out, then they will find us. Now get pulling.'

The two found a collection of leads and wires snaking their way in and out of the console and they began to tug and pull as hard as they could to disconnect them one by one, much to the amusement of a curious Byron. Unsure as to which lead would be most crucial to the lighthouse's operation, they decided to spare none. Some of the leads produced tiny sparks much to the surprise and laughter of Anwyn, who seemed to be revelling in the mischief.

'I think you are enjoying this a little too much!' joked Peter.

'There's nothing quite like buggering up technology. I think I have the taste for this now,' she said, yanking a stubborn red lead out of its socket. 'When we get back to the shore, I think I might plot the downfall of the entire technological world! Starting with the sodding toaster!'

Eventually all of the leads had been removed from their sockets, all of the lights went out on the console and the pips and beeps fell silent.

'Good job,' smiled Anwyn.

Peter looked at her and blessed her eyes with a kindly stare. 'Thank you.'

'What for?' asked Anwyn.

'You know,' he shrugged. No further words were needed, friends can say everything with their eyes. 'Just… thank you.'

Anwyn put her arms around him and placed a kiss, a tender kiss, on Peter's crown. 'No, thank *you*, Peter.'

14
Rescues

Back on the mainland, a little red light began to flash on a computer screen, in a non-descript office in the lighthouse control of an equally non-descript building. A little moustached man placed his thin-rimmed glasses on and squinted his eyes at the screen. He read the message *'Console Malfunction – Smalls Lighthouse'* aloud. His stubby fingers laboured slowly over the computer keys as he investigated the nature of the error. His jaw sank and his eyes widened as he scrolled down a list of technical errors caused by Peter and Anwyn.

'Bugger!' he said in a thin gravelly voice.

He dialled a number on his phone and tapped impatiently on the desk in front of him. Finally, a tinny voice responded, much to the man's relief.

'We have a complete technical malfunction at the Smalls Lighthouse,' said the man adjusting his glasses. 'Repeat! A complete technical shutdown at the Smalls Lighthouse. Investigate immediately! Repeat! Investigate immediately!'

The storm around the lighthouse had abated and now the waters were as still as a lily-pond in the summer. The sky above began to transform, as the whitening clouds began to permit rays of sunlight to shine hope on the two unlikely friends. As they stood outside on the balcony which ran the perimeter of the lighthouse, they began to see the world through brand new eyes. Although Anwyn knew that Michael was still *her* world, she now began to see that there was another world which, if she chose to, she could inhabit from time to time; a world of friendship and love. She also began to see that acknowledging that love did not necessarily mean leaving Michael behind. Indeed, she could relive her memories of Michael with her new friends. Likewise, Peter saw that not everyone in the world was a Kelly Moore or Adam Bargewood. There was kindness and love in St David's if only he could take his eyes off the fear, the pain and evil that *some* people are capable of. A kind of symbiotic realization had occurred. Both had shown the other the way, through an unlikely friendship and understanding.

The two watched the gannets diving like missiles into waves and marvelled at the little storm petrels skipping across the water, their wings inches from the surface of the water. On the rocks below, shags extended their dripping wings to dry in the emerging sun, while the gulls and terns created a cacophony which seemed at odds with the aesthetic beauty all around. In the distance the dorsal fins of dolphins would appear from time to time, as would the peeping heads of a pair of grey seals. Everything was profoundly beautiful.

Then, within the beauty came the relief. From out of the distance, emerging as a mere dot on the horizon, a boat approached. As it neared, its orange tones seemed to reflect the sunlight and it shone like a beacon. The boat drew closer and, as he squinted his eyes, Peter saw the figures of his parents holding on to the rail of the portside. There were no histrionics, no shouts, no calls for help, just two friends calmly looking out over the Welsh waters.

'I think it's time to go home,' said Anwyn, pulling her new friend into a warm embrace.

At the end of the longest of days, Huw sat on his son's bed. He looked around Peter's bedroom and, noticing posters that he had never really paid attention to, realised the extent to which he had missed a large chunk of his boy's childhood. He also noticed that the cuddly toys had been replaced by natural history books and National Geographic magazines. He couldn't help thinking that his son should be reading *The Beano* or *The Dandy* in his tender years and he could not forgive himself for not noticing the transition from child to young man. As his son curled up in his bed following a steaming bath, Huw looked at him with pride and a renewed and concentrated love.

'You do know I love you, don't you?' said Huw.

'Yes,' replied Peter, 'I know… now.'

'I didn't really… I wasn't really…' Huw stuttered. 'I never really said it, did I?'

'They're just words,' said Peter with a hint of irony.

'No,' said Huw, 'they are *the* words. They are the words that we should save for those who mean the most to us.'

Peter sat up and took his father's hand. He took in a deep breath and looked straight into Huw's vulnerable eyes.

'Did you…' he hesitated. '…Did you ever say that to Emma?'

Huw's heart broke a little more, leaving a scar that would never completely heal. 'No.' He squeezed his son's hand tightly. 'No, I didn't. I love your mother. I always have.'

'Then why did you do it?'

'I don't know,' said Huw. 'Emma was hurting, she was alone and I couldn't see someone like that so... so unhappy. I cared for her, I still do. She is a good person. She's not a villain in this story. There *are* no heroes or villains, just casualties. She deserves to be happy, we all do. But no, I never loved her. Not like that. We both just got confused.' Peter offered a half smile to his father. 'I know that's not the best answer, but it is the only one I have. I know I have let you down, son. I know it's going to take a long time to put things right, but I will. I *will* put things right... if you let me.'

Peter reached out and embraced his father with all he had. Huw held his son as if it the first time, with tenderness, care and pure unadulterated love. He stood up and turned out the bedroom light. He was just about to leave the room when Peter called him back.

'Dad?'

'Yes?'

'Are you mad about your boat?' asked Peter.

Huw paused for a moment. He looked at his son with a face much sterner than moments earlier. He sighed and shook his head, his brow furrowed.

'Nah!' he said 'It was a piece of shit!' Peter laughed aloud, the first time he had done so for a long, long time. 'Insurance to the rescue!'

Huw closed the door and made his way across the landing to the master bedroom. Maggie was drying her hair in a negligee which followed each and every curve of her exquisite body. Huw looked at her for a moment. Maggie noticing this, turned off the hairdryer and looked into her full-length mirror at Huw's reflection.

'What is it?'

'Nothing, I am just looking at you,' he said.

'Why?' said Maggie, through a gentle blush.

'Because I love you.'

Maggie smiled at him softly, 'Ditto!'

Huw turned his wife away from the mirror, picked up her hands and pulled them to his lips. He wanted to kiss the soft lips which he saw in front of him, he wanted to wrap his arms around Maggie, but he knew what was at stake. He proceeded with caution.

'We are scarred, aren't we?' he said. Maggie gave a smile of warmth, yet sadness. 'And I know I have to take responsibility for that. And I will. But scars heal, they don't go away... but they can heal.' Huw planted the softest and most tender kiss he could on Maggie's china-white cheeks. He paused on her cheek, long enough to smell her and listen to her gentle breaths.

A couple of days passed. The world was not perfect, but there was a renaissance of happiness and hope in St David's. Anwyn, Huw, Maggie and Peter all felt that such a rebirth would, with a little trust, hope and love, mature into the happiness they all deserved. Even the prospect of Peter's hearing at the child magistrates' court couldn't dim the light of optimism which now began to shine. Huw and Peter had spent the previous day working on a surprise that they had been preparing for Anwyn. The task gave father and son the first chance to work together for years. They heard each other's laughter as if hearing it for the very first time. They looked at each other through different eyes. Maggie had taken Anwyn shopping to buy some new clothes. Anwyn's austerity had extended to the same attire she had worn for decades and now was the time to treat oneself. Money had never been an obstacle, primarily because she had rarely put her hands into her pocket for anything other than books, which were always second-hand. After a long day of retail therapy in Cardiff and a pleasant lunchtime of tea and Welsh Cakes, Maggie and Anwyn pulled up outside the old girl's cottage.

'Oh, I must have left the lights on,' said Anwyn, observing the soft illumination extending out of the front window.

'No,' replied Maggie, 'I saw you turn them off when we left this morning.

Anwyn looked a little perplexed, not to say somewhat concerned. 'Well, then who is that in my house?'

Maggie smiled at Anwyn. It was a smile of mischief but also a smile of love.

'What are you grinning at, you silly sod?'

'Just you wait and see.'

'What do you mean?'

'Just be patient you old bugger,' said Maggie, 'We have got a surprise for you.'

Anwyn's smile reappeared. 'A surprise? For me?'

'Yes!' giggled Maggie.

'Well, if it's a stripper, you can bugger off now and leave me alone with the poor boy. I still remember the moves, you know.'

'I'm sure you do,' said Maggie, 'now hurry up and get out of the car.'

Maggie, laden with shopping bags filled to the brim with Anwyn's new ensembles, ran ahead and dropped the items just inside the front door, then returned to Anwyn. Just as they arrived at the doorstep, Maggie called out.

'Okay,' she said, 'turn out the lights!'

Despite the relative darkness, Maggie placed a hand over both of Anwyn's eyes and guided her slowly into the room.

'Well, let's be honest,' said Anwyn, extending her hands, trying to feel her way into the room, 'it's not going to be a surprise party, is it?'

'No, it's not a party.'

Anwyn was guided into her arm chair. She could hear whispers and the sound of the curtains being drawn.

'This is starting to get a little disturbing now,' she joked.

Finally, Maggie removed her hands. 'Okay,' she said quietly, 'you can look now.'

Anwyn's gaze took a while to focus in the darkness. In front of her she saw a large white square. As her eyes started to adjust, she saw that it was a large screen, beneath and in front of which was a projector connected to a laptop computer.

'Okay, Peter,' said Huw's voice, 'play the film.'

Anwyn looked to acknowledge Peter and Huw. She offered them a perplexed look, then Huw pointed at the screen.

'Don't look at me!' he said. 'Watch the screen!'

Slowly, fading from a pitch black background, Michael's face began to emerge from the darkness, not just a static photograph, but movement too. She watched as she saw her husband walking along the beach in Norfolk on a cold winter's day, twenty years previously. Her face turned to stone, every muscle in her body froze in an instant. She was suddenly completely unaware of everything around her. She couldn't see the teary face of Maggie or hear Byron's rat-a-tat feed on the wooden floorboards. The screen had no periphery; it was as though the rest of the world had simply disappeared. She watched as Michael wrote his name in the sand with a piece of driftwood. As he wrote in long swirling joined up letters, she heard the sound of the waves in the distance coming through speakers at either side of her chair. Then, her soul was stirred, her heart ignited and her mind revitalized, as she heard her husband's voice; the voice she had longed to hear for so many years, the voice she had tried to reconstruct in her mind during so many lonely nights, the voice that gave her a reason to get up in the morning.

'Michael, my love!' she said, beneath shallow breaths. 'Oh, my dearest Michael!'

She watched as Michael joked around by the waves, chasing the outgoing wavelets, only to be pursued in return by the incoming tide. She listened to his quirky high-pitched cry as the icy waters caught up with him and began to laugh through tears that soon flowed like a cataract of salt water down the happiest of faces. In the background, music began to emerge. Her favourite piece of music, Gerald Finzi's *Eclogue for Piano and Strings* started to drift through the room. The romance of the rising strings and the delicate punctuation of the piano melody heightened the joy that arose in her heart. As she watched him clowning around on the shoreline she began to notice the scent of his aftershave, drifting once again around the room.

'I have so wanted to hear his voice again,' wept Anwyn, 'to watch him move, to see his smile... I... I don't know how to thank you.'

'There's no need to thank us,' said Maggie.

'I wondered where my slides went,' said Anwyn.

'I picked them up when I let Byron out while you were shopping,' said Huw. 'I remember you said you'd like to see them.'

'So Dad and I put this little film together yesterday,' said Peter. 'You told me once that Gerald Finzi was your favourite composer. I picked out one of his pieces, I hope you like it.'

'I couldn't like it more,' said Anwyn reaching out for Peter's hand. 'I love it.'

'Well, you watch the rest of the film,' said Maggie, 'while I make us all a cup of tea.'

Anwyn watched the rest of the film with a permanent smile of pure and total happiness. She laughed out loud and cried a river of tears, although the grief was overshadowed by the elation of seeing Michael again. He was still gone, she knew that. But she also knew that her love for him was equal to the extent to which she had grieved for him. She could have no more love for him, so, by that token, she could have no more grief for him. It was time to move on, and with new friends and the love they brought to her life, she knew she wouldn't have to move alone.

After her guests had left, Anwyn had little to do. Maggie had washed all the dishes, Huw had dried them and Peter had put them away, albeit in completely the wrong place. Byron lapped away at his water bowl to quench his thirst and let out an elongated belch.

'I beg your pardon?'

Anwyn saw the slides and film reels which Huw had

taken, in a small box on top of the radiogram. She picked them up and took them to her bedroom to return them to a place of safekeeping. She sat down on the bed for a moment, picked out a few slides and held them up to the light to see them in miniature. She smiled once again before reaching underneath her bed and pulling out a box of bits and pieces, some important, some not. It included coins from Italy, Germany, Norway and Greece and other places she had visited with Michael, a number of pens and pencils, some paracetamol tablets and one of Michael's old poetry sketch books. She picked the A5 book out to look at it. She had never paid much attention to his notes or his drafts of poems when Michael was alive. Her view was that to read through his sketches would be like finding out how a magician sliced his assistant in half, only to return her to normal. She had always believed that much of the world's beauty lay in its mystery. There was something beautiful about not knowing everything. However, on this occasion her curiosity won over. Wanting to look at Michael's scruffy handwriting again, she opened the book and saw notes, doodles, etchings, sketchings, titles, words in circles and words crossed out. She noticed familiar lines here and there, rhyming couplets, sections of alliteration and metaphors, all separated from the verses that they would one day complete. She even noticed the signs of frustration and boredom, no doubt from a time when inspiration was not forthcoming; a little stick man had been crudely animated into the bottom right hand corner of each page. Anwyn flicked through the book and smiled to herself as she saw the stick man running. As she did so, a pack of folded A4 papers slipped from between the pages and landed on the floor at her feet. She bent down and retrieved the sheets. Then, rubbing her tired eyes, she started to read. The letter was addressed to Peter's former publisher in London and was dated two weeks before Michael's death.

Dear Harry

Please find enclosed the selected poems for consideration for publication under the pseudonym, Jack Newton. As stated in our recent telephone discussion, I feel I need to release these poems under another name, as they are far removed in style and content to that of my previous work. My existing audience may not wholly welcome this change of direction.

Kind regards

Michael

Anwyn froze. How could it be? Michael had never mentioned writing under a pseudonym. How could it be that the poems she heard coming out of the radiogram speakers were those of her dead husband? They were unpublished works so how did they escape out into the public? How did they find their way onto the poetry programme? Anwyn stood up slowly and walked back into the living room. Each step seemed to take a lifetime, each blink of her eyes seemed to fill her world with darkness for an hour and every breath she took in and breathed out seemed never-ending. Eventually, she stood before the radiogram and looked at it from every angle. Finally, she flicked the power switch. Nothing. She turned the switch on and off a number of times, but still no sound came out from behind the fabric of the speakers. No soft illumination appeared from behind the radio dial. She gave the side of the device a hard bang with her hands and tried the switch once more. Still nothing. With a lump in her throat and her pulse beginning to race, Anwyn began to pull the radiogram away from the wall and to her great incredulity she saw that the power lead had no plug. The lead, which extended a few inches from the back of the radiogram, ended with scruffy twists of copper wiring. It hadn't worked for years.

Still holding Michael's unpublished poetry in her hand, she slumped to the floor. All of a sudden the world seemed to make sense. Her confusion dissipated with the warmth of realisation and understanding. She looked at the poems in her hand, many of which she had heard on the radio, and once again felt the gentle heat of a joyful tear emerge from her eye. All those long dragging days, all of the lonely nights, while she wanted and needed her husband... he was there. Every time she heard a word of comfort or counsel come forth from the radio, the reason she had connected so deeply with the poems was because they were Michael's words. She looked around the room, half expecting to see him standing beside her.

'It was you, wasn't it?' she said through another tear, gathering, like dew, on the tip of her upper lip. 'You were there all along, weren't you? You sneaky little bugger!' She wiped her face with the palm of her hands, then swallowed. 'So... where are you now?' she suddenly became a little anxious. 'Why can't I hear the radio? Where have you gone? Michael? Michael, please! Don't go again.'

Suddenly a gentle force within her seemed to take over her head and hands. She felt compelled to pick out one of the poems and read it. The verse which came to hand was titled, *When Love is Silent.*

> *I hear your echoes call for me*
> *Across the void of time and space.*
> *But I have to be silent, my dear*
> *And have faith in your strength and grace.*
>
> *That I do not answer you*
> *Says nothing of my love.*
> *This paradise is nothing,*
> *Until you rejoin me above.*
>
> *But there is work to do*
> *And you must make a start.*
> *For there is still great strength*
> *And love within your heart.*
>
> *You need no stars to guide you,*
> *No compass showing north as true*
> *You still have a story to tell, my love*
> *And a world to tell it to.*

Anwyn knew that Michael was gone, and this time there would be no coming back. There was no need. Maggie, Huw and Peter had given her life a renewed purpose, a reason to get up again, a reason to see another sunrise, a reason to live. It made no sense, but then again, it made perfect sense. All that she had believed about spirituality, about life and death, was now open to intense scrutiny. But none of that really mattered any more. As she sat exhausted, slumped on the floor with tears running down her face, she felt like she had shed her skin. The grief, which had smothered her for so long, was lifting with every breath, like a delicate net curtain catching the softest breeze. Life was beginning again and, within the renaissance, within the magic and the mystery, within all of the things she would never have believed, she could, at last, see a clear road ahead.

A few weeks later, as the antidepressants began to kick in, Anwyn's memory began to improve, as did her love of life. Her profound friendship with Maggie, Huw and most notably, Peter, had given new meaning to her life. One white-skied morning, Huw called at her humble abode with no explanation and told her to wear something warm.

'Now?' she asked.

'Yep,' replied Huw, standing in the doorway.

'What about Byron?'

'Bring him along.'

Anwyn smiled. 'You really are a man of mystery, aren't you? Have I got time to put my face on?'

'Nope,' replied Huw, 'I'm afraid not. The one you're wearing is just fine.'

Anwyn placed her warm coat on, wrapped a long woollen scarf around her neck and fixed a rather embarrassing bobble-hat to her head. With an expectant smile on her face she followed Huw out to the car.

Ten minutes later she found herself at the boat launch, where Maggie and Peter were waiting, also wrapped up warmly. They stood next to a brand new motorboat, acquired by Huw courtesy of a surprisingly generous insurance payout. It was a large open top vessel with room to accommodate fifteen. On this occasion, however, it would take only four.

'Well,' said Huw, his face beaming with pride, 'what do you think?'

'It's fabulous!' exclaimed Anwyn.

Huw extended his hand to Anwyn and she held on tight as he helped her aboard. Maggie jumped on too, followed by Peter who wrapped Byron in his thick winter coat.

'Where are we going?' asked Anwyn.

'We're going shopping up the high street,' said Huw comically. 'Where do you think we're going? We're going out on the waves!'

'Why?'

'Because we're going to change your opinions about dolphins,' said Peter.

That afternoon, as the Ellis family and Anwyn bobbed about on the uncharacteristically placid waters around St David's, they laughed, joked and talked in an open and honest way that only true friends do. The natural world seemed to come out to celebrate their friendship. Bottlenose Dolphins, Grey Seals, as well as various breeds of porpoise and sea birds seemed to accompany them on their journey. Even a passing Minke Whale passed by, spurting water loudly into the air, much to the surprise of all. As Anwyn watched the playful dolphins leaping and diving through the water, she laughed and smiled as though she had never seen them before. It is strange how beautiful the world can seem through eyes that have found love and happiness, how sonorous the world can sound to ears which have heard laughter once more and how the heart can be so elevated by true friendship. Grief is ongoing but, over time, it diminishes, its pain less acute, its darkening shadow fades to grey; but only with love. And love also goes on, but with the help of time and friendship, gets stronger and, undeniably, *real*. The tides may wash grief upon one's shore but the tides will take it away again, and the next tide may bring all that we really need – love.

JACK NEWTON

Selected Poems

A Different World

The rays of the sun seem weak and diluted,
The rivers flow, slow, like sludge, polluted.
The rain does not soothe me, it cuts through to bone,
I feel a nagging breeze that won't leave me alone.
I can't see the beauty in this place anymore –
Did you take it all with you when you closed life's last door?
At least, love, I know when it's my turn to walk through,
I'll be greeted by the riches of wonder and the beauty of you.

Click

I often wondered how that moment might be,
Then all was revealed the day you left me;
When white turned black and day became night,
When muscle, bone and sinew gave up the fight.
At first I gauged nothing, there was nothing to see,
No sense that a loved ghost was leaving me.
I wanted some recognition, something profound.
Then I heard a click, an inauspicious sound.
But now looking back I know this to be true –
The sound was my heart, breaking in two.

The Angel - Ode to a Nurse

You were purer than heaven, your love was complete,
I watched how you soothed my dying mother's feet.
I could see this was so much more than a career -
You held my mother as if she were yours, tender and dear.
You could tell by her face that her time had come,
And you saw it in our eyes as we stood watching, numb.
But never have I felt so blessed by a smile,
Your eyes made the moment easier to reconcile.
There was nothing you could do to keep death at bay,
But with your hands, not wings, you saw Mum on her way.
You were the conduit from one world to another,
And I'm filled thanks for you - the angel who cared for my mother.

Do The Dead Grieve

As they sent you on you way, as the velvet curtain drew,
I wondered if you grieved for me, as I do for you.
I wondered if you cried for me in another place
Or if you could see the tears fall through the lines in my face.

Did you sing a song to remember me?
Did someone read a verse shakily?
Did someone hold your hand as they did mine?
Did someone tell you it will all be fine?

And those with whom you are now reunited,
Who did attend? Who was invited?
Auntie Pam and great-uncle Stan?
Did they gather around you and offer their hands?

But it doesn't seem fair somehow
That, as we grieve for one right now,
You mourn a congregation of hundreds and more,
Family and friends, with their heads to the floor.

I like to think that the grief is what binds us,
We hold together with the love that defines us.
It's a hand which reaches to where you may be,
And reminds me that somehow you are here with me.

Grief *is* Love

The grief doesn't stop with the last fallen tears,
It doesn't end when you stop counting the years.
It goes far beyond night-black attire,
Beyond flowered graves and cremating fires.
 And though you may not stare at a photograph,
Or try in vain to recall the sound of her laugh,
The grief remains, as so it should,
For grief is pain, but grief is good.

It reminds us that the love was strong,
And what's more, that it carries on.
Grief and love are the same, entwined like two lovers;
Grief is love and love is grief, you can't have one without the other.

A Child Can Tell

My black dog approached and proceeded to bite,
I was left crying alone in the night.
Then I heard a gentle tap on the bedroom door,
"Are you okay, Daddy?" ...
    "I'm fine."
       "Are you sure?"

The child could tell that this kind of weep
Was not so conducive to a good night's sleep.
So he pulled back the covers and climbed into bed,
Held me in his little arms and kissed my head.
In the morning I awoke and he was still there,
With such tenderness, such humility and such care.
So, if a child can perfect a love so true,
Perhaps, just perhaps, we can too.

And Yet...

When the wildest winds of the winter rattle the latches,
You bolt the heavy door and search for the matches.
You strike the strip and spark up a flame,
And you are sure that somehow you heard my name.
Yet, you will not believe.

When the shining hues of autumn turn your path gold.
Your soul is young and tender, but the bones and sinews old.
You feel a breeze cut through you and shiver in the cold,
And hear echoes of sweet musings you were told.
And yet, you will not believe.

In spring the birds sing sweetly from within the flowers bloom,
While you are pacing circles in a dark and lonely room,
You'll feel a touch upon your shoulder and turn around to see
An empty space, a dusty place and an outline of me.
And, yet you will not believe.

While the summer sun shines softly you're hiding in the shade
Recounting lover's promises that in earnest were made.
Then you'll lay some flowers on my tended grave
And swear on your life you could smell my aftershave.
And yet you will not believe.

But one day you will just let go and in faith you'll make the leap.
You'll close your eyes, look for me and breathe me in deep.
And in belief you'll see me, and the sight will not deceive,
For believing is seeing, and in seeing you'll believe.
And you *will* believe.

Love Doesn't Cease

Love doesn't cease with a lover's last breath,
It's stronger than life, it's stronger than death.
Love doesn't end with a one-sided hold,
There's warmth in the heart, though the body turns cold.
And love isn't over when it leaves the earth;
It shines from another place, proving its worth.
Love doesn't stop because you can't see it done,
 It labours on strong, in the memory of your loved one.
So should you feel alone, as you no doubt do,
Remember those who left, never left you.

The Lighthouse

Rising from the salt and surf
Through the Westerlies ire.
Standing stoic but so quiet,
And never to tire.

Turning shafts of guiding light
Will guide you home again,
Through all the gods may throw at you
To soothe your every pain.

And somewhere deep inside you,
The lighthouse rises strong,
Illuminating you with love
Through days dark and long.

And how it came to be there
Or how it came to shine,
Should not concern you friend.
Just know that all is fine.

Stars Turning Blue

A few shallow breaths slow down to a stop,
The bedside monitor gives one last hop.
Now all that is left is sinew and bone;
The woman who raised me, and praised me, is gone.
My father kisses the love on whom he doted,
While I recite a poem, Dylan Thomas quoted.
My brother is silent, my sister is screaming.
I blink my eyes hard and hope that I'm dreaming.
Indeed, I wake up, but alas the dream was true,
And I've lost my mother again, beneath stars turning blue.

Jon Lawrence

Unwelcome anniversary

Forget all the tinsel, the gifts 'neath the tree,
I do not want anything to remind me.
Silence the carols, silence the choirs,
Turn out the lights, extinguish the fires,
Unplug the TV, unhook the phone -
This Christmas I want to be alone.

When she left, she took the bright lights and colour
And left me here grey, in a world getting duller.
Where the melodies sound hollow and fake,
No art or symphony can soothe my aches.

And as for *You* up there on high,
As real to me as a pie in the sky,
Know that I despise you, for to pain you imparted,
To one on this earth who was golden hearted.

Hocus Pocus

All that hocus pocus and hippy ballyhoo!
Oversized mediums saying, "someone's coming through!"
Limp-wristed psychics with messages from the departed,
Tea-leaf readings? Tarot cards? Don't get me started!
And what a load tosh the astrologists say -
I'd have found pure happiness but "Saturn got in the way!"
All that tish and nonsense 'bout father, son and holy ghost.
But do you know what really irks me the most?

...I need it to be true.

I need to believe in something to make sense of the grief.
Where can you put your faith? Where do you put belief?
Or else it just means nothing, nothing at all.
Someone tell me why? Why do our loved ones fall?

Jon Lawrence

Knowing Where To Look

There's nothing in a jacket,
Left hanging on its hook.
Nothing between the faded pages
In the my favourite book.

You'll find no trace of me, dear one
Near the cufflinks in my drawer.
My aftershave may hold my scent
But, I fear, little more.

So take to the old LPs,
The golf clubs from the shed,
They're little more than *things*.
Mourn no longer for me... I am dead.

So look now to the future.
You have a brand new start.
I'm not in the dip on my side of the bed,
I'm deep within you... in your heart.

Let Their Arms Embrace You

Let their arms embrace you
Though they may not be mine.
Let their loving heal you
And, in their love, be kind.

Let them see your every face,
Let them see your tears.
Let them hear your laugh and cries,
Give voice to all your fears.

Don't push their hands away,
They may take away your pain.
Let friendship be the summer sun
To grief's winter rain.

Some Memories Linger

Some memories linger,
Some come and go.
Some last a lifetime,
And some you can't hold.

You might rightly ask
Why you should recall,
The sound of footsteps
Echoing down a hall.

Yet there's no room
In your mind to rejoice
A sweet memory of
A lost lovers voice.

You can't pick or choose
The things you remember.
Which nephew's birthday
Is the fifth of December?

But the memories that matter
All are made clear,
With ashes to ashes,
When the next world is near.

Arrangements

The body has barely lost its heat,
They haven't even placed the tag on her feet.
And yet, the mind runs three steps ahead,
Barely acknowledging that a loved on is dead.

What colour flowers? What type did she want?
What message for the gravestone? What font?
What kind of coffin? Ebony? Natural? White?
And, of course, make sure the music's right.
No mournful hymns, Satchmo will do,
What a wonderful world - such a beautiful tune.

Order the church, speak to the priest,
Give him the info about 'the deceased.'
Select the pallbearers to carry her in.
What time should the service begin?
And of course, who will read a eulogy?
Which readings, prayers or poems to read?

Speak to the caterers, sort out the food -
Something light and easy, a buffet is always good.
Who to invite to the church and the wake?
Keep Aunt Ethel away from Cousin Jake.
It'll be a long day, wear comfortable shoes.
Keep Uncle Terry away from the booze!

So when do I mourn? When do I cry?
When do I really say my goodbye?
Can I hold myself together until then?

Do what mum said, "Just count to ten."
No doubt one day, the pain will arrive,
To remind me of your death... but remind me I'm alive.

A Year in My Room

You left in the spring, the flowers didn't bloom,
So I hid away from the world in my dark little room.

Summer brought lithium heat but I was still cold,
So I'd lie on my bed and dreamt of your hold.

In the autumn no leaves fell soft on my head,
I pulled the sheets over me and wept instead.

In the winter the long, dark nights suited me.
I covered my aching head, 'til I could barely breathe.

But then the spring came, with hope once again,
And with hope comes a reason to live, a cure for the pain.

So it's time to open the curtains, let life in and shout.
Open all the windows, and let the grief drift out.

Explanations

How do you explain to a child as he holds your hand,
Things that even you don't understand?
How do you start to make sense of it all,
To the child weeping on the stairs in the hall?
And in between each butterfly breath,
Somehow you have to explain this thing called, death.

Do you use words like sleeping or perhaps, 'at peace,' -
That Grandma is free from pain, she has been released?
Do you tell him that heaven is there, that she is on a cloud?
Looking down and watching over him, that she's very proud.
Do you share your belief that there's nothing there -
That grandma has vanished into the air?

Do you teach your child to close their eyes -
Be blind to their grief when someone dies?
Do you tell them to cry as much as they need -
What advice can they possibly heed?
For all he knows, when their little life turns black,
Is that Grandma is gone and she can't come back.

But some how they work it out, with or without you.
They have the resilience of character, that you used to.
The answers they give themselves may not be right,
But they may serve to make their black world bright.
So, in conclusion, there really is nothing to say,
All they need is love for them to find their way.

Internal Illuminations

I'm sure that Freud would have much to say,
About my loathing and hatred for this thing we call, 'day.'
But what, I am sure, would interest him more,
Are the reasons the daytime makes me so sore.

You see, in the day I live on my own,
In this lifeless place we used to call home.
I wander in stupors, neither here nor there.
I don't want to be and I don't want to care.

But the nighttime arrives and in dreams you return.
Memories stir and deep passions burn.
Then the dawn chorus comes and sings you away
And leaves me alone in the darkness of day.

I'm bitter that daylight brings such nugatory thoughts;
I am angry, resentful and somewhat distraught.
Do the shopping, the cleaning, pick the kids up from school.
I tell them I'm fine - who am I trying to fool?

I can't wait for the moment when it all turns black,
And in the place of my dreams - I have you back.
I can smell you and taste you and feel you again.
I can hear your sweet voice sing a lilting refrain.

But such illuminations I know, one day must end
In the kindness of family and warmth of good friends.
But just for tonight, love, illuminate bright,
And hold me again in the stillness of night.

When love is silent

I hear your echoes call for me
Across the void of time and space.
But I have to be silent, my dear
And have faith in your strength and grace.

That I do not answer you
Says nothing of my love.
This paradise is nothing,
Until you rejoin me above.

But there is work to do
And you must make a start.
For there is still great strength
And love within your heart.

You need no stars to guide you,
No compass showing north as true
You still have a story to tell, my love
And a world to tell it to.

ABOUT THE AUTHOR

Jon Lawrence, a novelist, playwright, poet, musician and teacher from South Wales, lives in the east of England. He studied at Leeds University, Sheffield University and Nottingham Trent. To date he has published two novels (*The Pastoral* and *Playing Beneath the Havelock House*), two novellas (*Albatross Bay* and *Bisha*), a collection of poems (*Moetapu*) and a play (*The Wallflower Café*). He has also written three musicals for school children. As a musician he has released a number of albums in an array of genres.

www.jonlawrence.org

www.facebook.com/jonlawrencewriting

Playing Beneath the Havelock House

The Wallflower Cafe

Albatross Bay

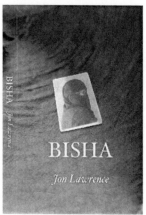

Bisha

The Pastoral

Moetapu